HALLOWEEN PARTY MURDER

JUNIPER HOLIDAY COZY MYSTERIES BOOK 1

LEIGHANN DOBBS

CHAPTER ONE

*J*uniper Holiday was so excited about hosting Crescent Cove's creepiest, scariest, most fright-inducing haunted house for this year's Halloween party, she'd called her nearest neighbor, Fedora Layhee, to show up before the horde of guests arriving this evening... just to make sure everything exceeded even the stingiest expectation.

She loved all things Halloween and was an avid horror fan. If anything was amiss, Fedora would know.

As the wealthiest patron on the east side and also possibly the west side of Crescent Cove, Juniper found special delight in hosting the biggest, best celebrations the Cove had ever seen. To get an invite to one of her "shindigs," as she called them, was coveted among all the Covians. Everyone wanted to see what Juniper Holiday would think up next, and she made it a goal to always surprise them.

This year, she'd commandeered her own guesthouse to create the Haunted Hangout, a haunted-house feature that would be in addition to the main party going on in the mansion. It was going to be an absolute fright. She'd even borrowed a real coffin from the town mortuary to lay out the dead in style. Fedora was currently inspecting this coffin under the watchful eyes of the three resident cats, Ludo, Loki, and Finn. Finn sat atop the casket, his luminescent green eyes watching their every move. Ludo was sniffing Fedora's shoes with her dainty pink nose, and Loki sat in the corner, grooming his fluffy black tail.

Fedora struggled with the latches then pushed up the top, causing Finn to jump to the floor. "Oh my, how realistic! And it's not just the makeup, either, although whoever is responsible for that has done a remarkable job. Look, Juni. Feel this skin! See what I mean? So cold! And the veins, and the translucence of her skin… It's so pallid. I love it!"

In front of the open coffin, Fedora turned to Juniper and squealed with obvious excitement then clapped her hands together in quick succession, a wide smile on her face. "Oh, Juniper, you've outdone yourself this year. She really looks dead!"

Juniper peered over Fedora's shoulder at the coffin, blinked, did a bit of a double take, then pushed her way forward. She'd hired an actress named Dorella Smith to pose as a corpse who would jump up and scare people at opportune moments, but Juniper had no idea she'd already arrived. She'd play the part perfectly, though, with her eyelashes that looked like spider legs, four-inch-long black fingernails, and pasty white skin, and that was even before makeup. Juni had also hired a makeup artist to enhance her ghoulish look.

Juniper brushed her brown curls out of her eyes and nudged Fedora to the right. She wanted to look at the finished product. "Move aside so I can get a closer look."

Juniper gasped. The makeup artist had done

a fantastic job. The body didn't even look like Dorella. Wait, maybe it wasn't Dorella.

"Dorella?" Juniper waited for an answer, but there was nothing, not even an eyelash twitch.

Juniper had a very bad feeling about this. She reached out and touched the body. "Darn! I think she's really dead!"

"Oh!" Fedora's eyes went round. "Oh, dear. Juni?"

Ignoring the woman, Juniper tightened her lips and sighed. "If that's who I think it is, she's not even supposed to be the one in there."

Juniper leaned closer to the body, her eyes narrowed, as she studied the ghostly corpse. There was a row of scratches along her left cheek and what looked like a bruise on her neck. But what happened to her, and how in the world did she get in the casket? Juniper was sure the casket had been empty earlier that afternoon when she met with Randy at the funeral parlor to pick it out. "Tori? Tori, come here."

Turning, she waved her goddaughter over. Tall, slim, and blond, Victoria Cooper had lived with Juniper exclusively for the past ten years. Her parents, killed in a car crash, were once

Juniper's dearest friends. After their deaths, Juniper had taken Tori in and treated her as she would have her own daughter. Tori was an adult now, but she and Juniper were as close as hot dogs and mustard and loved residing in the same house. And the mansion was plenty big enough.

"Tori, call 911. Send everyone waiting outside back up to the main house then wait here for the detective to arrive. Looks like the party will have to be contained in the house." Juniper surveyed the elaborate decorations that had taken days for her to put up in the carriage house. "Such a shame too. It looks fantastic in here."

Victoria frowned. "Is something wrong?"

Juniper pointed at the coffin. "This is not the corpse I hired for this evening's festivities and not an actor a'tall. I believe this lady is Hannah Peterson from the Peterson-Jakes Mortuary and Funeral Home in town."

"Oh my God, you mean she's actually dead?" Fedora squealed and simultaneously jumped away from the coffin as far as her sixty-year-old legs would allow. Her eyes closed, and she visibly swallowed. "Oh, I touched a dead

5

body—a real dead body! Juni, I think I might be sick."

"It'll be all right, Dora," Tori said. Still, she turned to her godmother with eyes gone wide. "You can't leave me here with all your guests arriving and a... a dead body! Where are you going, Juni?"

Juniper had already fished her keys from her purse and was headed out the door to the garage. "You'll be fine, Tori. You and the others can keep the guests busy at the mansion until I return. Turn on some music," she said, giving a wave of her hand. "People love to dance."

Victoria pulled away from a now-trembling Fedora and followed her godmother from the guesthouse to the spacious six-car garage on the other side of the fountain in the center of the wrap-around drive. "But where are you going?"

Juniper slid into the soft leather bucket seat on the driver's side of her brand-new candied-apple-red Mustang GT—the only car currently in the garage—and pressed the ignition switch. Queen's "Bohemian Rhapsody" blared into the relative silence, and she reached over and lowered the volume a bit before turning back to her goddaughter. "Did you see the scratches on her face, Tori? I need to pay a visit to the werewolves."

A frown touched Tori's brow, and she cocked her hip, one hand resting there and the other holding open the car door. "A few scratches don't automatically incriminate the werewolves. They aren't the only creatures in town with claws, June."

"Yes, but there was also bruising on her throat as if someone had choked her," Juniper said, putting her hand to her own throat and grimacing. "Excuse me for saying this, but I don't think the goblins are that strong, dearest."

Tori was not impressed.

Juniper sighed. "I'm just going to ask some questions. Nothing more. They may have seen something. You never know. At the very least, I might warn them."

Tori narrowed her eyes.

Juniper cocked a brow.

Tori sighed loudly and rolled her eyes. "Fine," she said, taking her hand off the door and crossing her arms. "Just don't go causing any trouble. I like it here, and I don't want to get kicked out."

Juniper closed the door as she put her hand

on her chest. "Me? Cause trouble? Dear, who do you think I am?"

Tori didn't get a chance to answer as Juniper revved the engine and sped away, jauntily waving at her while disappearing down the drive.

"Juniper Holiday is who I think you are," Tori muttered, shaking her head. "And that in itself means trouble."

CHAPTER TWO

*D*espite the party happening at the Holiday mansion, Rarely Done, the local steak house, was packed to the gills. That wasn't unusual, though. Rarely Done was one of the most popular restaurants in the area. The only time the place was empty was when it was closed. Juniper was fond of the porterhouse, and their barbecue was to die for. But that wasn't why she was here.

"Hey, Juni, I thought I heard your screamin' demon! What are you doing down here? I thought your big shindig was happening tonight?"

Juniper looked in the direction the voice had come from and found Garrett, a big, burly man in his mid-thirties with a voice to match his physique, making his way toward her. She noticed more than a few pair of eyes following him—and so did he, winking at one of the female customers just to see her blush.

It was all in fun. Everyone knew Garrett was a big flirt, but more than that, he was a giant teddy bear with an equally giant heart.

That he was a werewolf was something only Juniper and Tori knew, having seen him shift beneath the full moon some years ago. They were sworn to secrecy, of course, and they'd kept their promise.

"It is," she answered. "I ran into a snag, though, and thought I might swing by to ask some questions."

"Sure," Garrett said with a nod. "Whaddaya need to know?"

"What I need to know is best not talked about in mixed company," she hedged, giving him a look.

Garrett frowned. "Pat's manning the grill, but I can throw Victor on, and we'll meet you in my office in three?"

"Sounds good," Juniper said, flashing a grin.

With that, she made her way to the back and through the thick oak door marked Staff Only on a gold placard. There was a short hallway that led to the kitchens, and she could hear the sounds of food cooking and staff barking orders back and forth, no pun intended. But she went to the door on the right of the hallway that had Management stamped in bold letters on another placard. She turned the knob and went inside to wait.

Two minutes later, Garrett stepped inside, followed by another fellow of slighter build but no less impressive. Pat, or Patroclus as he'd been named at birth, nodded when he saw her, his eerie light-blue eyes shining with tempered concern.

"Juni. Garrett says you've got trouble?"

"*We* might have trouble," she corrected, looking back and forth between them.

Garrett sighed, went around, and sat behind his desk. He rested his arms atop the glossy cherry wood and said, "All right, what's going on, June?"

Juniper pursed her lips. "Well," she began, "someone was found murdered in the haunted house, and judging by the marks on them, I think the killer wanted it to look like maybe one of you guys did it."

"Why?"

Juniper went on to explain the bruising on the throat and the scratch marks on the face.

"That doesn't automatically point fingers in our direction," Pat said, frowning. "Anyone could have done it."

"The scratches were rather claw-like, if you get my drift," Juniper said.

Pat narrowed his eyes. "Hardly anyone in this town knows about that except you and your goddaughter, Juniper. So unless you've been talking it's still a big secret. Besides, we don't kill people, and frankly, I'm offended that you would insinuate something like that."

"I'm not insinuating anything," Juniper said, rolling her own eyes. "I'm trying to warn you, you stubborn wolf. But I guess I wasn't being clear enough." She huffed out a sigh. "Someone else could have found out your secret and, for whatever reason, decided to blame their crime on you."

"Impossible. We keep our secret very close," Garrett said, giving Juniper a hard look.

"And Tori and I still found out."

Pat scoffed. "That was because you and Tori were trespassing on our lands. You never would have found out if you hadn't been skinny-dipping in the lake."

Juniper shrugged. "You gotta break some rules every once in a while. Besides," she said, flashing a grin at Garrett, "we weren't the only ones naked in the lake by the end of it."

A red flush filled Garrett's cheeks, and he cleared his throat. "We're not discussing that at the moment." Focusing his gaze on Juniper, he continued, "Are those the only incriminating marks, Juni?"

"As far as I know," she said. "I didn't exactly examine the body as thoroughly as a pathologist would. I saw the marks on Hannah's face and neck and thought I might need to give y'all a heads-up in case word gets out about your monthly activities."

"Thanks, June," Pat said. "We'll keep an extra eye out and a few more ears listening."

"Let me know if you hear anything," Juniper said, standing to leave.

"You be careful too," Garrett said, standing and walking around the desk.

"Whatever for?" Juniper asked, frowning up at him.

"Because, Juniper Holiday, that body was found at *your* place. Maybe whoever killed the victim is trying to frame you and not us."

"Fudge buckets," she grumped. "I didn't think of that." She clicked her tongue. "That does change some things."

She frowned, wondering why she hadn't made that exact connection herself. And here she had run off to town after the body was found and the detective was on the way. Not the best light to paint herself in in this instance.

"We've got your back if you need us," Pat said, putting his hand on her shoulder and giving a reassuring squeeze.

"Thanks," she said, giving him a quick smile. "The same goes for you guys. Howl, and I'll come running as fast as I can."

"You've got to stop with the wolf puns, June," said Garrett, walking out with her.

Juniper just laughed.

Once she was in her car, she turned on the radio, and Ozzy Osbourne's "Bark at the Moon" came blaring through the speakers. She laughed again, knowing certain folks inside would be able to hear it. Then she backed out of the parking spot and sped back to the mansion, hoping she got there before Detective Mallard did. Handsome as he was, that man was a jar of green olives on top of lemons, and she was not looking forward to seeing him.

CHAPTER THREE

*D*esmond Mallard stretched himself slowly from the front seat of his sedan, unfolding his height while his dark eyes scanned the area the cops had already taped off, missing nothing. Everything seemed exactly as it should. Nothing out of place, the guest lane neatly roped off at both entrance and exit from the haunted house Juniper had set up. No screaming teens, no dragging ne'er-do-wells skulking in the shadows of the hedgerow, and yet the 911 operator had informed him this was the sight of a ghastly murder.

At least the crime scene hadn't been trampled by partygoers. He was hoping at least for a scuff mark or two. Signs of a broken entry.

Something to make his job easier. His eyes scanning every movement, Desmond started toward the guesthouse, since the lack of evidence out here suggested all his clues lay inside.

"Desi, you're here." Victoria Cooper's deadpan voice met him on the other side of the door, which she'd opened for him before he knocked.

"Victoria," he acknowledged with a slight nod. "Where are the guests? Is this not tonight's attraction?"

"Not anymore." Tori shook her head and motioned him forward to the center of the entryway, where the victim's body lay. "The coffin we arranged to borrow from the mortuary came with an unexpected occupant. Juni had me call you guys right away."

"She's not here?" he asked, immediately latching on to what Tori hadn't said instead of what she had. *Clue number one*, he thought. *Witness fled scene of crime.* "Do you know when she left? Where did she go? What time is she expected back? This is her party, after all."

Clue number two, he added to the mental list he'd only just begun. Potential suspect or accomplice possibly going off to warn the guilty party.

"She—ah, she had to pick up some things for the ghouls. Fake blood. She should be here soon," Fedora offered. "Can I go now, Detective? I really need to get into costume before the music starts."

Desmond's eyes narrowed. "You were here too? When the body was found?"

Suspect list, Desmond thought. Juniper Holiday, eccentric billionaire with a flair for the dramatic. Check. Victoria Cooper, eccentric goddaughter of Juniper. Check. Fedora Layhee, neighbor. Critic. Weirdo lover of the dark things. Check. Double check.

Fedora rubbed her hands together and nodded. "I was here, yes, but only because Juni called me. She wanted me to do a walk-through, you know? To make sure things were properly terrifying for tonight. She asked me to give her my worst so she could make this Halloween the absolute best to date."

"And?" Desmond asked, sure she had more to add.

"And I was the one who actually opened the

coffin." She shrugged and looked at the floor. "I guess that means I found the body."

Possible suspect or accomplice number two? Desmond added to his already growing mental notes. Fedora Layhee discovered the body. "Yes. Yes, Ms. Layhee, it does. I'll need you to stay put for now. Do not leave the guesthouse. I'm sure I'll have more questions for you later."

To Victoria, he said, "You'll need to make a list of everyone who's had access to the guesthouse for this party."

Tori winced. "Everyone? But, Detective, a lot of people have been in and out. Decorating. Painting. Setting up props."

"Everyone. Including yourself, Ms. Juniper, and all the regular staff," Desmond confirmed. "If someone's been in here in the past two weeks, I want to know about it, whether it's the electric company or the party planners. List them all. You can use the table right over there where the bowl of eyeballs currently sits. Stay here, Miss Cooper. I'll have more questions for you too."

"But, Mr. Mallard, I've got to go back to the mansion! Everyone will be arriving soon, and if

I'm not up there to greet the guests, Juni will have my head!"

His eyes narrowed again. "Well, then she will be the main suspect in two murder cases. Isn't that right, Miss Cooper? I don't think she would dare. Do you?"

Recognizing a trick question when she heard one, Tori kept her mouth shut about it. Her own eyes narrowed to thin slits. "Very well, Mr. Mallard. You'll have your list shortly, though I don't see why your black-and-blue-suited minions can't do some simple bank-statement-checking detective work and make the list on their own. They can find anything they need to know about everybody by following the money —including that Dorella Smith was supposed to be in that coffin tonight instead of the Peterson-Jakes funeral director. Juni paid tonight's actors weeks in advance. The bonus was supposed to come after."

Bonus pay for a crime well done? Possible and noted. Desmond nodded. "I'll put someone on that right away, Miss Cooper. For now, I'd like to see the body."

CHAPTER FOUR

Flashing blue lights greeted Juniper as she rolled up the mansion's drive, and she sighed to herself. She had only moments to brace herself for what was sure to be a thrilling meeting with Desmond Mallard.

She had rather hoped that stiff-necked fuddy-duddy wouldn't be here yet, but seeing his very boring sedan next to the marked police cars drowned that hope lickety-split.

"Ma'am, you can't come up here," a young man called out to her.

A second later, someone else responded. "That's Juniper, Ackers. This is her place."

She smirked to herself. *Ah, he must be new to*

the Cove. Everyone else knew her by the sound of her car alone.

When she got out of the car, she made her way to the guesthouse, where Sour Mallard was no doubt waiting for her. The answer presented itself in a pristine gray pin-striped suit and black tie as Desmond opened the door to the guest-house and stepped to the side to allow her to walk past. There wasn't a wrinkle on him, she noticed. Not even a strand of his pitch-black hair was out of place. Darn it if he didn't remind her a bit of the Pierce Brosnan version of James Bond. Too bad he wasn't anywhere near as fun.

Grinning wide, she greeted him as she swept by and inside. "Desi! How nice of you to drop by. Are you gonna stay for the party?"

"I don't think there will be a party, Ms. Holi-day. Or did it escape your notice this is now a murder investigation?"

Out of sight of Mr. No Fun, Juniper rolled her eyes. "Of course it hasn't," she said, turning back to face him. "And I do feel sad for the deceased. But nobody said we couldn't have a party at the same time. Ooh, you know what would be fun? If we got the guests involved! They could help solve the murder! It would be—"

"Disastrous," said Desmond, his tone flat. "I will not have dozens of people traipsing through my crime scene, fouling up the evidence."

"Hundreds," she corrected. "I don't have small parties, Detective Sourpuss. They are always big and loud."

"I'm sure," Desmond said, his shoulders going back slightly as his chest filled with a breath.

Juniper could swear she saw a tic start in his jaw. Just how badly could she fluster him, she wondered?

"He's in a mood, Juni," Tori said from somewhere in the room. "I wouldn't waste my time if I were you."

Juniper looked and found her sitting cross-legged on the table in the exact spot where the bowl of eyeballs had been. Tori's hand was flying across a piece of paper. "Are you taking notes for your next story?" Juniper asked, walking over to peek at the paper.

Tori snorted. "I wish. No, Desi wanted a list

of names of everyone who's been in and out of here. He seems to be against doing his own research."

Juniper hummed. She spun on her heels and turned to face Desmond again. "Have you at least taken a look at the victim, Detective?"

"He did," Tori answered for him, sounding almost bored. "Opened the casket, barely blinked, then closed it again."

"Has the coroner been here?" Juniper asked, going over to take another peek in the casket, only for Desmond to thwart her .

He put his hand out to keep her from touching it. "I wouldn't if I were you," he warned.

"I was just going to see if maybe I could see something you hadn't. Two pairs of eyes are better than one and all that."

Desmond shook his head. "The only thing you are going to do, Ms. Holiday, is answer questions. The body doesn't need to be further contaminated."

Juniper's brows rose. "It's contaminated?"

"He means don't touch it, Juni," Tori offered, still scribbling.

"Well, I wasn't gonna do that. That'd be gross. Cold and clammy. Yeesh," Juniper said with a shudder. "No, thank you."

"Ms. Holiday, what were you doing in town tonight?"

"I went to pick up a few last-minute things for the party, Detective."

She actually had stopped to get a few things after visiting the wolves. Those items were all still in her car.

"Go check the back seat if you don't believe me," she told Desmond, pointing over her shoulder with her thumb.

"And you thought it necessary to purchase party supplies right after you found a body?"

That did seem a bit callous, didn't it? Juniper probably should have thought that out before she flew off. Well, what was done was done.

"Technically, Fedora found the body," Juniper said then frowned. "Speaking of Fedora, where is she?"

"Don't worry about Ms. Layhee right now, Ms. Holiday. Why—"

"Desi already questioned her and sent her

home," Tori interrupted, hopping off the table to join them. She thrust the papers in Desmond's direction. "Here you are," she said. "There are enough names on that list to keep you busy for a little while, I think."

"Thank you, Miss Cooper," Desmond said, taking the papers. He folded them in half and slid them in the inner pocket of his suit jacket.

Tori nodded and rocked back on her heels, sliding her hands in her back pockets. "If that's all, I'm heading back to the main house. There's a cupcake or five calling my name, and I need to make sure things are set. Guests are arriving."

She patted Juniper on the shoulder before she turned and walked out.

"Mmm, cupcakes do sound good," Juniper said, turning to follow her goddaughter.

"We're not done here, Ms. Holiday."

Juniper spun on her heel again to face him while walking backward to the door. "Oh, but we are, Detective Mallard," she said. "I'll give you the guesthouse. No party here while you do your crime-scene thing. But the main house is far enough away, and nothing happened there. So unless you have a reason to detain me further, we are very done here."

And with that, she turned back around and walked out, mentally keeping her fingers crossed that he didn't call her back.

CHAPTER FIVE

Still staring at Juniper's departing back, Desmond Mallard gritted his teeth. The woman thought she could do anything, and from what he had seen since she'd moved into Crescent Cove, she was mostly right. He'd never seen a woman with as much energy as Juniper Holiday seemed to have—especially not at her age. He would almost go so far as to say she amazed him sometimes, but he felt that would be seriously pushing his entire response to her, so he refrained.

Not that Juni ranked high on his list of people he intentionally paid attention to. Until tonight, she'd mostly played in the background of the Cove's upper-society social fabric. Her goddaughter, Victoria, however, rarely seemed to accompany Juni on her most flamboyant outings, and he couldn't figure out why. Since she'd reportedly taken Victoria in when her parents died, wouldn't it make more sense if the two spent more time out and about together?

"Maybe they do, Detective, but you're not around to see it. Not that you'd want to be, given Juni's presence and all, but we all know you're quite interested in Miss Tori."

Desmond's eyes flared, and he spun around. The small hairs on his wrists and the back of his neck stood on end. Did he just hear a voice?

No one else was in the room. His associates were going over the grounds for clues, and Victoria was right earlier—he had sent Fedora Layhee home. Nobody besides Victoria and Juniper had entered the guesthouse since. So who had spoken to him?

Looking around, he caught the glint of something in the back. A pair of eyes! No, three pairs. Who was back there? He started toward them when three cats bolted out of the shadows.

"Meow!" They scattered out the door toward the mansion.

Well, that explained it. Not entirely, though.

Cats didn't speak human languages, and he was sure he'd heard something… or had he mistaken purrs and meows for words? Maybe he had been working too hard.

Turning in a slow circle, Desmond searched the room for a speaker. No doubt Juni had an intercom system set up somewhere that she intended to use to scare the bejesus out of her guests. Of course that must be it. She would love to have another person corroborate her outlandish stories of ghosts haunting Holiday House, but he silently vowed he would never be that person. But who was talking to him through it, and how did they know what he had been thinking? Lucky guess?

"Who's there?" he called just in case and then began a slow stroll around the main room. He poked his head into an open doorway on his right. Nothing. The one on his left yielded the same.

He spun around and then froze, thinking he saw something small move on the floor over by the casket, but there was nothing. Probably his imagination.

After making a complete patrol of the ground floor, he reached up with his right hand to rub at the back of his neck. The short hairs lay down, but the edgy feeling someone else was there with him despite his being deserted by his chief suspect did not. "Ackers! Haverman! Get in here! I want the entire guesthouse swept for comms, top to bottom, inside and out. I'll be outside, waiting for the coroner. Let me know what you find, but don't touch anything without gloves."

"I'm pretty sure none of the furnishings will be wearing gloves, sir," Ackers pointed out as he walked by.

Desmond almost choked in response to the man's sarcastic, utterly unfunny comeback.

"What the—?" He reached out and halted the man. "Just because we are in her domain does not give you leave to act like Ms. Holiday, Stuart. Feel free to persist in such nonsense if you must, but know I'll have no compunction against your taking early retirement if you do. None whatsoever."

The minute he stepped outside, loud music belting out of the mansion assaulted his ears. The drive was filled with vehicles, as dozens and dozens of guests had begun to arrive for the Holiday Halloween bash—a party to which he himself had not been invited. Not that he wanted to be.

He spun on his heels and headed for his car. He'd start his report while he waited for the coroner to arrive.

Glancing once more toward the vehicle-filled drive, he searched for one with a coroner label emblazoned on the side. At least a dozen cars were ahead of it, all slowly creeping forward to the mansion. He opened the door to his own vehicle and slid into the driver's seat.

"Haverman, get me next of kin for Hannah Jiles Peterson."

"Oh, so the body has been identified?" came the reply.

Desmond's lips tightened. "Just get me what I asked for and quickly."

"Yes, sir, Mr. Mallard."

Questions, always questions, Desmond thought. When would he finally get a team who knew protocols and procedures and... well, and him? This pair had been with him for more than half a year, and yet they still questioned his actions, though not usually this casually.

He looked up at the dark sky, noting how the clouds moved slowly yet still glided eerily across the light of the full moon. Was it simply because tonight was Halloween that things seemed to be off? Or was it the location of this particular crime?

Eyes narrowed, he peered at the mansion on the hill, aglow with light and practically vibrating on its foundation from the beat of the music. He decided then and there it was her. Juniper Holiday. She made people go off the rails on a regular basis, and tonight was no different. The woman was trouble, and once this case was done, he promised himself, he would make a point to steer clear of both her and her outlandish parties.

Through the warm light of the large windows, he could see every costume from witches to princesses to superheroes with capes. A flapper in a pink-and-silver dress caught his eye. Was that Victoria?

Maybe he should enter the party and listen to the gossip mill. By now, the place should be abuzz about the murder. And if people started talking about visiting the guesthouse and messing up his crime scene, he wouldn't hesitate to shut things down.

CHAPTER SIX

Once inside, Juniper hurried upstairs to her room. The guests were already arriving, and here she was not in costume!

She closed the door and began undressing. A moment later, a sonorous male voice intoned, "Shall we get rid of the detective, ma'am?"

Juniper laughed, completely unconcerned that someone was in her room. It wasn't like she could keep him out, anyway. As a ghost, Lionel could pass through any wall and door he wanted in this place, and no one would be able to stop him.

"That won't be necessary, Lionel. I think Desi Dearest has earned his right to be here tonight. So long as he doesn't interfere with the party proper, he can stay."

Her decision received a haughty sniff, and she turned to Lionel as she toed off her shoes, her brow arched. "What?"

"Nothing, Madam Juniper," Lionel said, his back to her. Even in death, he was conscious of people's privacy. Juniper wouldn't have cared if he stared at her butt-naked, though. She was completely comfortable in her skin. A body was a body, and everyone had one.

"It's not nothing, Lionel," she said, padding barefoot over the plush carpet to her canopied four-poster, where her costume was laid out. She pulled on the white dress shirt, buttoning it to just shy of truly scandalous. "That sniff means you have an opinion but don't want to say what it is."

"Madam, I—" Lionel began, his tone implying her words were insulting.

"Out with it, Lionel," Juniper said. She walked to the antique dresser set against the far wall and plucked a pair of original Wayfarers from it. "I'm decent. You can turn around now."

He did so, looking at her in a way that

implied he thought she wasn't in possession of all her faculties but didn't want to risk his position by saying so. Not that he was in danger of being fired. Lionel, like the other ghosts on the property, was here for better or worse, and it seemed tonight was for worse, since there was a dead woman in her guesthouse.

"Detective Mallard does not seem the type to let things lie, especially not when it comes to his job," Lionel said. "He will harass your guests if you let him wander about as he pleases."

"We're not going to let him wander about, Lionel," Juniper said with a smile and a shake of her head.

"*We* are not, ma'am?"

"You heard me the first time. I think Jacobi, Lissy, and you can keep him in check for a few hours, don't you?"

A great, bereaved sigh came from Lionel's lips. "Of course, madam."

She flashed him a big grin. "Thank you."

Another few minutes passed wherein Juniper freshened her makeup and put a short brunette wig on so she would look more the part. *Joel Goodson wished he looked this good in* Risky Business, she thought, winking at her reflection in the mirror.

As she turned to leave, she found that Lionel was still there.

"Is there a problem?" she asked.

"Only the body lying in the guesthouse, ma'am."

A frown pinched Juniper's brow as she thought. "Did you or any of the others see what happened, Lionel? Was poor Hannah Peterson *murdered* in my guesthouse?"

Lionel shook his head, his ghostly hair waving behind him. "No, ma'am. Miss Fletcher, Mr. Oakes, and I were all keeping an eye on things whilst it was being turned into a house of horrors for tonight's festivities. No one was murdered on our watch. We only popped out for a few minutes to see to things in the main house."

Juniper put her hands on her hips and bit her bottom lip, worrying it between her teeth as she thought. "That means she was already dead and in the coffin when it was delivered. And that was *hours* ago," she said with a shiver. "I like fake dead things, not real ones—present company excluded, of course."

Lionel made no comment.

A moment later, a series of rapid knocks sounded upon her door. In an instant, Tori opened it and stuck her head in. She was dressed as a flapper with a pink-and-silver shimmery beaded dress, a string of long beads down to her belly button, and a pink-and-white feather atop her head. She looked gorgeous.

"Are you ever going to get yourself down-stairs?" she asked. "People are starting to look for you."

"Sorry. I was just talking to Lionel," Juniper said, hopping on first one foot and then the other as she pulled on a pair of tube socks, the last bit of her costume.

Tori's eyes widened slightly. She slipped inside the room, closing the door behind her. "About what?" she asked, looking around for signs of a ghostly presence she could not see.

"The dead body currently occupying space in my guesthouse," Juniper said on her way to the door, dragging Tori out with her. "He says neither he, Jacobi, nor Lissy have seen anything, and they were in the guesthouse, keeping an eye on things," she explained as they descended the stairs. "So the body had to have been in the coffin when it got here."

"That is both sad and disturbing," Tori said, making a face.

Juniper nodded. "Yes, it is."

"But how did she get in the coffin?" Tori mused.

"She did work at the funeral parlor. Maybe she fell in. Pretty convenient place to end up dead, though."

The closer they got to the ground floor, the louder the music became. Juniper patted Tori on the shoulder as they turned a corner and headed into the main party area. "We'll talk about this later," she said. "It's almost time for my grand entrance. Oh, and keep an eye out for Detective Mallard. I'm sure he'll poke his nose where he doesn't need to tonight."

"You let him in?" Tori complained.

"I didn't *let* him in," Juniper said with a roll of her eyes. "But I didn't tell him he couldn't come in, either. Just make sure he doesn't try to interrogate anyone, and the night should go off without a hitch—erm, aside from the dead body, I mean."

"You owe me for this, Juniper Holiday," Tori

muttered, shaking her head as she walked off into the gathering crowd.

Juniper snorted then raised her hand to wave to a couple of teens, a boy and a girl dressed as ghosts, who were oohing and aah-ing over the bubbling cauldron set up next to the food table in the large foyer. Another teen, dressed in a skeleton costume, stood farther back near the coat closet, watching the festivities. When they noticed her, they did a double take, eyes going wide at her strange outfit.

"*Risky Business*," she said as she walked by on her way to the ballroom. "Watch it. It's iconic."

Just like me, she thought, sliding her sunglasses on and popping her shirt collar as she got ready to greet her guests.

Tori cued the music, and Juniper slid into the ballroom amid raucous cheers.

But while she was busy entertaining, her mind was on the murder. She couldn't help but wonder if someone was trying to frame her. They could be in this very room, in fact. But who? And why would they kill Hannah?

CHAPTER SEVEN

*T*he unmistakable notes of "Old Time Rock and Roll" by Bob Seger and the Silver Bullet Band punched through the speakers, and every head turned to watch the spectacle in the middle of the ballroom.

The still-impressionable teens who'd come with their parents to Juniper Holiday's Halloween party weren't the only ones who studied Juniper with raised brows. Desmond watched the entire opening to one of the most iconic eighties movies play out before him in astonishing accuracy… astonishing because the character playing the lead role was female, but Juniper Holiday was just that kind of woman.

She didn't look half-bad in boxer shorts, either. Shaking his head, he headed into the crowd— and ran into Victoria.

"Oh! Detective Mallard! I didn't know you'd be joining us for the festivities!" she shouted over the music.

Desmond cut a glance in her direction. "Not exactly. I thought I would mingle with the guests, say hello, and find out if anyone here committed murder this evening."

Victoria laughed. "C'mon, Dez. You know they wouldn't tell you if they did. That's what your expert forensics team is for...finding out who did it despite what they say."

"You find it funny there's a dead body in your guesthouse as we speak, Miss Cooper?" he asked. He shoved his hands into the pockets of his suit jacket, but other than that, he showed no outward sign of the discomfort he felt. The house was filled with Juni fans. Victoria was Juniper's goddaughter, so she was also a fan. The only one not here to rave over the wonder of this evening and the lady responsible for their fun was him.

Someone nudged him from behind, and he

turned slowly to stare into Juniper's dark glasses. A slow grin spread her lips. "Dee! Desi! De-Mal! Glad you decided to come up and mingle a bit."

His brow wrinkled. "I'm not here for the party, Ms. Holiday. I only hoped not to disrupt it while collecting what information I could glean from your guests."

"Business schmoozing in a murder investigation?" Juniper's eyebrow arched over the top of her glasses, and she shook her head. "Good grief, Mallard. Lighten up! Get loose. Shake a few things. How long has it actually been since you last cut loose from the ice in your veins and had fun?"

Desmond stiffened. "I take my job seriously, Ms. Holiday. And, as I am sure you are fully aware, solving a murder is a most serious job."

Another song on Juniper's playlist broke into the air, inciting squeals and hoots from the dancers, and she, of course, began to sway to the rhythm as soon as the beat hit. "That's my cue, Tori, baby! I'm off. Why don't you see if you can get Mr. Dull and Boring here to relax?"

As her aunt melted into the crowd, Victoria looped her arm through Desmond's. She led him away a few steps toward the side of the large, lavishly decorated ballroom to where the food waited. "Of course, I don't find the murder the least bit funny. I feel terrible for the family. And we're certain you will figure out who stashed Hannah in that coffin. But right now, you should have a drink."

Upstairs, a meeting was taking place. Lionel, the esteemed Holiday butler; Jacobi, the once-renowned cook; and Felicity, the Holidays' ever-loyal housekeeper (though all three were now on the "other side" of living) had gathered around Ms. Holiday's desk to discuss the matter of the body in the guesthouse.

"I'm not a fan of that Mallard character." Felicity frowned. Ghostly light played with the contours of her face, reminiscent of someone holding a flashlight under their chin.

"He seems a bit full of himself. I'd like to take him down a peg," Jacobi said.

"I may have taken care of that." Lionel smiled at the thought.

"What did you do?" Felicity asked.

"Well, for one, I spoke up when he was talking to himself. Gave him a bit of a fright," Lionel laughed. "And for two, I've ensured that Juniper will one-up him in the clue department."

"Did you meddle with the crime scene?" Felicity looked like she was about to launch into a lecture on the pitfalls of meddling, so Lionel hurried to answer.

"I simply delayed the finding of a clue. I found something under the casket and whisked it away to a hidden spot so the detective and his minions wouldn't discover it. Later on, I'll put it somewhere that Juniper or Victoria will find it."

"Where?" Felicity asked.

"Perhaps under the corner of the rug in the back where I saw you sweep dust sometimes, back in the day."

"I never!" Felicity scoffed.

"Seems like no harm done," Jacobi said quickly to prevent their spat from escalating. "One of us should go down there and have a better look at the body before the coroner takes it away. I believe it should be you, Lionel. Felicity and I will mingle among the guests and listen to their conversations. Find out who is worried and who isn't."

"We won't get to the truth of the matter until later, however," Felicity volunteered. "When the truth serum has time to kick in."

Lionel gave her a look. "Truth serum?"

She grinned, a laugh bordering on a cackle falling from her lips. "Alcohol. Once the adults have a few drinks, their tongues tend to loosen significantly. I have high hopes for getting the juiciest gossip tonight, both about the murder and otherwise."

Jacobi had stared at Lionel throughout their discourse. He shook his head, sending ghostly tendrils of light shimmering about it. To Lionel, he said, "Some days I wonder where you have been hiding all these years."

Rather than dignify the man's words with a reply, Lionel simply vanished.

"I assume he's gone to the guesthouse to have a look-see," Felicity said as she floated toward the door. "Come, Jac. Time to mingle."

The cook held out his arm, waited for her diaphanous fingers to float above it, then looked straight ahead and did his best possible Duckie Dale imitation. "Let's plow."

Felicity's laughter floated behind them, mingling with the music as they made their way below.

CHAPTER EIGHT

$\mathcal{J}$uniper made good use of the off-limits rooms to get to the kitchens without having to stop and interact with anyone. In particular, she was trying to avoid Dorella Smith. She'd promised her a big bonus if she performed well as the corpse, but thanks to the actual corpse, Dorella hadn't gotten a chance. Juniper imagined the woman would waste no time demanding the bonus anyway. But she'd scanned the crowd as she'd performed and seen no sign of Dorella. Odd; she should surely be here by now.

Sabrina, her real-life live-in cook, was pulling a batch of triple chocolate cookies from the oven as Juniper slipped and skidded her way across the slippery tile floor.

Maybe it was a bad idea to wear socks with no grips on the bottoms…

"You better not fall and knock your head on this floor, Juniper Holiday," Sabrina said. "There will be enough fake blood to clean up after tonight. I don't think anyone wants to deal with the real stuff."

"I'm good," Juniper said, holding onto the countertop like a kid grabbing the side of a skating rink the first time on skates. She frowned. "Why are these floors so darn slippery, anyway?"

"They were cleaned extra good for the party," Sabrina answered, taking the oven mitt from her hand and tossing it to the side. She looked at Juniper, one brow cocked. "What can I do for you tonight, Juni Holiday?"

"Did you see anything strange happen in the guesthouse while things were getting set up?" Juniper asked, tapping her nails on the immaculate marble countertop.

Sabrina shook her head, making her long black curls bounce from her ponytail. "Can't say that I have. I've been in here all day. Why?" she asked with a frown.

"There's a real-live dead person inside the coffin in the haunted house, and now Detective Mallard and his ducklings are all over the place. The guesthouse has police tape all over it, and I'm actually surprised no one has mentioned it, seeing as how Desmond and his team were crawling over the place like ants when everyone arrived."

Sabrina glanced out the window. "I noticed. Maybe they think it's part of the party."

Juniper pursed her lips, her brow furrowing in a frown. "Something about this ain't right."

"You think?" Sabrina said after a minute, her brows lifted high. She sighed and folded her arms, and a look of sadness crossed her features. "Do you know who it is?"

"Who is what?"

"The dead person, Juniper."

"Right. Um, well, I'm pretty sure it's Hannah Peterson. At least, the face shape is the same, from what I remember," Juniper said, her frown deepening. "It's been a while since I've seen her, so—"

"A few hours isn't that long, Ms. Holiday," came Desmond Mallard's no-nonsense voice.

Juniper fought the urge to roll her eyes. It figured he would find her when she was trying to piece things together. She turned to face him. "Detective. I would say, 'What a coincidence,' but I know you don't appreciate my humor."

"It's hard to appreciate something delivered so tactlessly."

"I have impeccable tact."

Desmond's brow lifted slightly.

Juniper grinned, batting her lashes for effect.

Desmond turned his attention to Sabrina. "Ms. Lafferty, isn't it?"

"To you, yes," Sabrina replied, smiling.

Juniper attempted to cover her snort with a cough, but judging by the ill-disguised look of contempt that Desmond passed her way, she was unsuccessful.

She sighed. "Look, Detective, instead of trying to be surreptitious about what happened in my guesthouse, why don't we sit down and talk? We can start with the only fact we have: Fedora Layhee found the body in the coffin. When the body got there, no one knows. But we need to find out—and soon."

Desmond stared at her for a minute, his dark eyes seeming to bore into her—and then he laughed. It wasn't a mirthful laugh but one resembling a villain's dark chuckle. Juniper was almost surprised.

"Ms. Holiday, you are the last person I would discuss this case with. But I'll do you one better." He raised his wrist to his mouth and spoke into the mic there. "Ackers. Haverman. Shut it down."

And just like Hannah Peterson, the Holiday Halloween Extravaganza came to an abrupt and premature end.

Outside, the body was loaded into the coroner's van, and the doors were shut. Sequestered inside along with the cadaver, Lionel, unseen by the living, unzipped the body bag and leaned over the body, his face mere inches from the poor dead woman's.

A series of scratches, none of them particularly deep, ran the length of her cheek, ending at the corner of her mouth. Her neck showed signs of bruising, but he could not determine what was used to cause it. It didn't look like a handprint, though. That much he could ascertain. And was that a small puncture wound? Hard to tell.

Further inspection—and he had to hurry before the van left—revealed very little. She seemed fine aside from being dead. Too bad her ghost didn't pop up and tell him who had murdered her.

Lionel gave a ghostly sigh and straightened.

The back doors opened again, and a gurgling scream worked its way from the autopsy technician's throat, though the poor fellow tried to choke it back.

"Derrick, did you forget to zip this thing?"

"No, Tanner."

"Then why is it unzipped?"

"It's not—dude, what's going on?"

"I don't know," Tanner said, hopping into the van and zipping the bag closed once again. "Let's just get out of here. I don't like this place."

"Same," Derrick replied and started out of the drive.

But before they could clear the gate, Lionel

decided to slowly unzip the bag right before Tanner's very eyes.

Sometimes, it was fun being a ghost.

CHAPTER NINE

The next morning, Juniper was still fuming that her glorious ghoul-fest of a Halloween party had been shut down. Desmond Mallard had done the unthinkable, the most detestable, heinous, horrendous thing ever that night. He'd shut the party down. Now, every time Juniper thought of what had happened, her blood boiled all over again. "Oh, that man! I invited him in, offered him food, drink, and a good time, and what did he do? He sent everyone home—before midnight—and to top it all off, I can't find my pink silk scarf with the Eiffel Tower on it!"

Victoria barely looked up from her computer. She knew how much Juniper liked that scarf to fly in the wind behind her as she raced down the road in her car, but she had several of them. Juniper's anger was mostly directed at Detective Mallard. "You're furious with the detective, yes, I know. We all know."

"And I have a right to be!" Juniper insisted. "We didn't even make it to the witching hour, Tor! No Halloween party worth the name ends before the time of crossing over."

"Crossing over?" Tori's fingers stilled on the keys. "Do you mean your ghosts are gone?"

Juniper snorted. "Oh, for Heaven's sake. No, they are not gone. If they were, how do you think I would know that rotten man was headed for the mansion right now? Jacobi was floating around at the gate, and he saw the detective's car.

Juniper shuddered. "Well, if you can call that hideous heap of metal a car. Why does the man lack so much in the taste department? With looks like his, he could easily drive a '65 Vette. Or even a Lambo. But noooo. He chooses something sensible. A sedate, se-boring sedan!"

Realizing she was never going to get any work done while her godmother was in her current mood, Victoria switched her laptop into sleep mode and pushed her chair back. "Oh, so you've actually noticed the detective is a bit handsome?"

Juniper's face suddenly looked like she'd been forced to swallow sour prunes. "Handsome? That's your word, dear. I would have said he's kind of hot. Or smokin', even. You girls are as tame with your adjectives as Detective Duckman is with his car."

Victoria chuckled and walked to the window. Peeling back the heavy drapes, she saw that Jacobi—Juni's ghost cook—had been correct. The detective was getting out of his vehicle, but he must have forgotten something inside because he ducked back in to retrieve it. While trying not to notice the way his slacks tightened in a few places, Victoria said, "Jacki was right, Juni. He's out there in the drive."

"Of course he is. But why? I don't need him here. I don't want him here. Not after he ruined the best Halloween party ever to be held in Crescent Cove. Make him disappear, Tori. Please."

Letting the curtain drop, Victoria turned. "But what if he has information about Ms. Peterson?"

Juni replied with a dismissing wave of her hand. "Pshaw. He would never share that information with me, and we both know it. Still," she said, suddenly thoughtful, "there must be a reason for his visit. Felicity!"

Victoria tried to see the housekeeper of the unliving variety, but her squinting was to no avail. The woman had clearly appeared from somewhere, though, because Juniper continued to speak.

"Go down there and follow him up. If he mumbles or whispers, I want to know about it. Heck, I wanna know if he belches!"

Her orders given, Juniper hurried toward the stairs. "You meet him, Tori. I need to go upstairs for something I forgot."

"What would that be?" Victoria called after her.

"To not be down here when that man comes into my house again. It might be dangerous— for both of us!"

Victoria shook her head. "That woman won't do."

"Won't do what, Miss Cooper?" Desmond asked, clearly confused.

"Much of anything one expects," she told

him then waved him over. "Come in, Detective Mallard. What may I do for you today? Any news on the murderer?"

Upstairs, Juniper waited for Felicity to spill the beans. "Well? What did he say? Anything?"

The housekeeper shook her head. "Nothing, Ms. Holiday. He merely glided over the pavers right up to the door in that smooth way of his. He never said a word, though…"

The woman paused just long enough to let Juniper release a sigh of impatience. "Though?"

She smiled. "He did run his fingers through those thick locks of his just before he rang the bell."

Floating into a seated position, Felicity held out her ghostly hand as if to inspect her nails. "Personally, I think he's sweet on someone."

"Oh, for crying out loud." Exasperated, Juniper headed for the door. "I don't know why I even bother leaving the details to others when I know if I want something done—or discovered—I will have to do it myself."

At the foot of the stairs, she drew up quickly. Faced by both Victoria and the detective, who stared at her with a multitude of questions in their eyes, she glared back. "What?"

"The detective has a few leads, Juni," Tori said. "Forensics found a particular wound on Ms. Peterson's neck."

Juniper's eyes went wide. "Werewolves? In the Cove? Oh, for my next party…"

"Ms. Holiday, the injury was not inflicted by canines—neither the pet nor the human variety," Mallard offered, his tone flat. "Try again."

Trailing her hand along the banister as she finished her descent, Juniper said, "Why don't you just tell us, Mal?"

"It seems Ms. Peterson died of a venous air embolism," he told her.

"Embolism? You mean it was natural causes? And what… she just keeled over and happened to fall into the casket, and no one noticed before it was delivered?" Juni was incredulous at the possibility.

"Not likely, though maybe the killer might wish us to think that." Mallard eyed Juni, as if by "the killer'" he meant her. "We also found a tiny puncture wound in her neck. It's possible someone injected air into her artery in the exact right location that caused the embolism."

Juni clutched at her neck. "Ewww."

"And we know there must have been a struggle because of the scratches." Mallard's gaze slid to June's hands as if judging if her fingernails were long enough to leave the scratches in Hannah Peterson's face.

"Well, that leaves me out. I don't have any needles." Juni gestured to her youthful face. "Not an ounce of Botox is needed to keep this face looking young." *Not yet, anyway.*

"Right, well, my boys will be finishing up in the guesthouse soon, so we'll be out of your hair. And if I were you, I'd keep out of the investigation." Mallard nodded at Victoria and headed toward the front door.

"As if I would meddle in his investigation," Juni said under her breath. But, of course, she fully intended to look into things, especially since it seemed that Duck Boy had her name on his suspect list.

Juni checked her phone. She was expecting a message from Dorella Smith, demanding her bonus, but there was nothing very unusual. Juni then wondered if Dorella had access to hypodermic needles. Her fingernails were certainly long enough to cause scratches. And she was supposed to be in the guesthouse around the time the casket was delivered. But that was crazy. Dorella didn't even know Hanna, did she? And even if she did, what would Hannah have been doing in the guesthouse?

CHAPTER TEN

*J*uniper was still fuming over the detective's words days later. Why it even mattered to her, she didn't know. It wasn't like she was in his shoes, solving crimes and all that... except she would love to solve this one, if only to prove she could and that she could do it better than Duckaroonie —*and faster*. Oh, now that would really get him going.

She might be a suspect, and that would be a good reason to investigate. Not to mention that it had occurred to her more than once that someone might be framing her. Yep, all good reasons to take matters into her own hands.

Chuckling to herself, she rubbed her hands

together and trotted off to find Tori. Juniper nearly tripped over Loki, Sabrina's black-and-gray tabby, as she stepped off the last stair. "Ack! Lordy, girly, you have got to stop getting between my feet while I'm walking," she said as she bent down to pick up the cat. "You're gonna kill me. And given my luck, I'll be stuck haunting this place. Honestly, that might be fun, but I'm not ready for that yet, and I don't think the afterlife is ready for me, so let's call a truce, shall we?"

Loki meowed and butted her head against Juniper's chin, signaling she wanted to be petted and couldn't care less about Juniper's truce.

"You are so spoiled," Juniper mumbled around a smile as she gave in to the cat's demands. "We're gonna go find Tori, okay? If Barclay is in residence, I will, of course, put you down so you two can continue your eternal game of tag."

Loki simply purred.

Ducking into Tori's room proved it empty, and Juniper frowned. Tori was usually neck deep in words by this time of day. Where had she gone off to? Before she could leave the room, Barclay, Tori's beloved Jack Russel-and-

Chihuahua mix, stuck his head up from the pile of blankets in the middle of Tori's bed and gave a warning bark that was nothing more than a rumble of sound. And then he noticed Loki, and Loki noticed him, and Juniper put the cat down before she could claw her arms to shreds.

Loki took off, and Barclay followed, the sound of his claws ticking on the floor serving as a sort of tracker to his location, which was great if anyone ever needed to find one of the cats. Barclay always knew where they were, and if he didn't, he would find them.

Juniper padded into the kitchen, where Sabrina was busy preparing lunch. "Rina-bina, have you seen Tori?"

"She was in here about five minutes ago, filching chips out of the pantry," Sabrina said, chopping bell peppers with lightning speed.

"They're probably a sight better than whatever concoction you're brewing for lunch," Jacobi grouched, scowling as he watched Sabrina cut vegetables.

Behave, Juniper mouthed at him, giving him a warning glare.

Jacobi glared right back. "She is butchering the chicken-and-greens recipe my great-great-

great-grandmother perfected—*perfected*—thank you very much."

Juniper pursed her lips. She knew for a fact the woman hadn't perfected anything. The recipe was generations old and bland as water. Sabrina was truly doing God's work when she took a notion to play around with the old recipes that had come with the mansion.

Go find something else to occupy yourself with, Juniper mouthed, making a shooing motion with her hands.

"Is there a problem?" Sabrina asked, glancing at Juniper before putting the sliced and diced peppers into a bowl.

"No. There was a fly. Did, uh, did Tori say where she was going? She's not in her room, and I need to talk to her."

"She is in the guesthouse, madam," Lionel intoned, floating into the kitchen via the north wall.

"Thanks, Lion-o, you're the best," Juniper said aloud, snapping her fingers and making finger guns at him as she walked backward out of the kitchen.

Sabrina, used to Juniper's strange shenanigans, just shook her head and continued preparing for lunch, unaware of the ghostly cook scowling at her from across the room.

Barefoot, Juniper made her way across the yard to the guesthouse. The police tape had been removed, and Detective Mallard and his duck gang had long since stopped tromping all over the place, looking for clues that weren't there. At least, Juniper assumed there were no clues. She didn't visit the guesthouse often unless she had a reason to.

"Victorino," she sang as she opened the door and stepped inside, "you in here? Sabrina said you were."

"Over here," Tori said, waving her hand to catch Juniper's attention.

"Yep, I see ya," Juniper said, walking over. "Listen, I had a great idea earlier, and I wanted to run it by you—what in the heck is that?"

"I believe it's an iron-on patch," Tori said, frowning at it. She looked up at Juniper. "It doesn't belong to anyone here that I know of. Looks like a band logo or something. I'm not familiar with it, though."

Juniper frowned. "Why would it be—" She stopped mid-sentence, her eyes going wide.

"Holy smokin' Joe's. How much you wanna bet that belongs to our killer, Tori-babe?"

"Uh, none," Tori said, frowning at her. "And what do you mean *our* killer? We're not trying to find anyone."

"Actually, we are," Juniper said, snatching the patch from Tori's unsuspecting hand and examining it. "That was what I came to talk to you about. We're going to solve this murder before Mister Waddles can."

Tori exhaled loudly and rolled her eyes. "Detective Mallard doesn't waddle."

"No, but ducks do, and he's named after one. Unh-uh! Hush. Only thing I wanna hear out of you is that you're in," Juniper said, holding her hand up when Tori was about to interrupt.

Tori scowled and crossed her arms. "We could get into trouble."

"That's a given, yes. Also, what's the point if it's easy and safe? That's boring."

Tori glared at her again. "We should give this to the police. It's odd they didn't find it. It was right there under the rug. I practically tripped over it."

Juniper shrugged. "I guess they aren't very

competent. If you aren't in, I can solve the murder on my own."

"That's the dangerous part," Tori said, rolling her eyes.

Juniper grinned. "So you're in?"

Tori gave a tired sigh. "Like Flynn."

"That's my girl."

CHAPTER ELEVEN

*J*uniper settled in at a computer table at the Crescent Cove library and opened up a half dozen browser windows. Sure, she had internet at the mansion, but she didn't want this search to be on her computer just in case the police decided to come looking.

In one browser window, she looked up the mortuary-slash-funeral home. In another, she opened the home page of the band featured on the iron-on patch Tori found in the guesthouse. In a third, she ran a search on Hannah Peterson herself. If it had information she could read, that would be great, but Juni was really hoping to find photos.

The remaining browser windows she used to check up on Victoria's book reviews across various sites. Not that Tori ever did. Tori insisted she wasn't writing for those reasons. She was only writing books so she could read the kind of stories she wanted to read instead of the ones some marketing firm paid their band of reviewers to tell her were the good ones.

A quick scan of Tori's latest release showed it already had hundreds of reviews, mostly positive, but it had only been released a week ago. Fans—real ones—were raving about it. Juniper smiled. Smart people! She personally loved everything Tori put out, but it gave her warm fuzzies to see she wasn't the only one. After that, Juniper turned her attention to research.

Hannah Peterson was in her late forties, was raising a stepson—Gage—who was her late husband's child. Hannah had no children of her own. She'd worked at the funeral home for the past twenty-three years. Dedicated to her job. There were a few pictures, but they were only pro shots from the mortuary website. Juniper was looking for more personal ones. She closed the mortuary page and opened a new one to search for the stepson.

As expected, she hit a gold mine on social media.

Gage Peterson was seventeen and had graduated high school a year early, with honors. He enjoyed water sports and owned a jet ski but had no employment details that she could find. His girlfriend, nineteen-year-old Brandi Hulsey, was going to nursing school and was apparently into music and the local band scene. Local bands—ha!

Juniper clicked on some of the images and enlarged them. Gage was tall with medium-brown hair. He looked rather sullen in most of the pictures, but then, a lot of teens did. Brandi was shorter with bright-purple-and-white hair. Apparently, she liked band patches. She had several ironed onto her jacket, even one that looked just like the one Tori had found in the guesthouse.

While dots connected in her thoughts, she closed the window and quickly scanned the band page for whatever pertinent info she could find. Were they involved in activism? Did they have beefs with women who worked with the dead? No, not that she could see. Closing the band window, she opened another and searched for local band news, gig news, anything. She found concert dates but still no leads.

But wait! What was this? Deep in the search for Hanna, a little news article appeared. Apparently, Hannah had had an altercation with someone in the parking lot of Rarely Done that resulted in a police call. And the someone she'd had the altercation with was none other than Dorella Smith!

The altercation had occurred months ago, but Dorella seemed like the type to hold a grudge. What if Dorella had shown up to play her part and run into Hannah, and they argued? Maybe Hannah dropped dead, and Dorella panicked and pushed her into the casket. Could the puncture wound just be a coincidence? Maybe the embolism really was natural.

But why would Hannah even be at the guesthouse? She worked in the admin part of the funeral parlor, but maybe she wanted to oversee the delivery of the casket. Surely there would have been other witnesses, though, and how would Dorella inject air into Hanna's artery to cause the embolism?

Juniper still hadn't heard from Dorella,

which was odd in itself. Perhaps it was time to pay her a visit.

Juniper closed the browser entirely and grabbed her purse, intent on pursuing the connections she'd made. Dorella had argued with Hannah, and the two of them may have been in the guesthouse together. The patch Tori found led to a teenage girl who happened to be dating the stepson of the dead body that had wound up in her guesthouse. Did that little girl kill Hannah? Somehow, Juniper didn't think so, but she still needed to ask some questions and get some answers.

Three blocks later, she walked up to the counter of Vinyl Tape, Crescent Cove's local music store. "Yes, I'd like two tickets to tomorrow night's Lyrical Larynx concert—it's at the park, yes?"

The clerk told her it was and gave her the tickets, and after a quick tap of her wallet on the payment screen, Juni headed out again with a grin on her lips. "Tori is going to love this!"

Across the street, Desmond Mallard keyed the mic at his collar and said, "Follow her. If she stops anywhere else, I want to know immediately."

"Yes, sir, Detective Mallard. As for what she was doing in the music store, she picked up a couple of tickets for tomorrow night's concert in the park. Think she has a date?"

Desmond felt sorry for the guy if she did. "I assume she will be treating her goddaughter, but we won't know for sure until we see for ourselves."

"We have to show up in uniform at the concert, sir? Won't that draw attention?"

Desmond barely refrained from rolling his eyes. "We aren't planning an attack. I'll be in plain clothes, and you'll be dressed as extra security. Our presence won't even cause a ripple."

"Oh! Right, sir. Gotcha. Okay, she's in her car. We are heading out."

This time, Desmond nearly gave in to the temptation to roll his eyes but quickly reined in such nonsense. "I will meet you back at the station. I have a bit of research to do."

Before he could carry out his plan, however,

he needed to find out why Juniper Holiday had suddenly decided to patronize an upstart local band. She knew something—he was sure of it. Juniper knew something she wasn't telling him, but he was determined to know.

Something about finding himself going head-to-head with Juniper Holiday was almost... satisfying. Strangely enough, he was enjoying his job more right now than he had in all the several years after his first as a detective. He found a challenge in facing her, outwitting her—and he would outwit her. He just had to figure out how.

CHAPTER TWELVE

*D*orella Smith lived in a small ranch house in an older neighborhood. The houses were all on small but neatly maintained lots. Dorella's house was white with green shutters and a one-car garage. There was no car in the driveway, but Juniper figured she probably parked in the small attached garage, so she pulled in, got out, marched to the front door, and rang the bell.

She thought she saw movement through the window next to the door and started to mentally prepare her line of questions, but no one came to the door.

"Dorella! It's me, Juniper!" Juniper knocked hard.

No answer.

"I know you're in there!" Juniper cupped her hands around her face and peered through the window. She didn't see anything moving. Perhaps it had been her imagination, or maybe Dorella had a cat... or maybe Dorella was hiding out because she'd killed Hannah.

Or the woman simply wasn't home. The garage didn't have a window, so Juniper couldn't see if her car was in there.

She turned away with a sigh, pulled out her phone, and left Dorella a message to call her right away.

This was probably a dead end anyway. The patch, she was sure, was the real clue. They always said that the close relatives were the first suspects in a murder, and that patch pointed directly at Hanna's relatives. Maybe she didn't like Gage's choice of girlfriend, and Brandi took exception to that. The girl liked band patches, and she was in nursing school and would know exactly where to place that needle.

Lucky thing Juniper had an idea of where she might be able to learn more about who owned that patch.

Juniper's next stop was not home, as one might assume, but the steak house. Why? Because she was hungry, for one thing, and for another… wolves had good noses. She'd made sure to tuck the patch into a plastic bag and put it in her purse before she left the house for this very reason. There could be something on it that an ordinary person wouldn't be able to pick up on.

She parked her car, which currently had "Nobody's Fool" by Cinderella playing at very high decibels, and killed the engine, which in turn killed the music. A few heads turned her way, some watching with humor and others shaking in disappointment. Some people got it, and some didn't.

Juniper threw her blue silk scarf in the back seat. She'd practically torn the coat closet in the foyer apart and still could not find the pink one. It was really irking her.

With her short brown curls blowing in the wind, Juniper strode across the lot to the steak house. She pushed her sunglasses on top of her head when she stepped inside. It smelled heavenly, and she was in the mood for a feast.

Ursula and Whitney, two of the human waitresses who worked there, smiled and waved at her as she walked to a table and sat down. But it was Victor, a werewolf, who took her order: New York strip medium rare and a baked potato.

"Is Garrett or Pat in today, Vic?" she asked when he returned with her drink.

"Pat is." A look of mild concern touched his face. "Is everything okay?"

She nodded. "Everything's peachy. Will you tell him I need to talk to him about something before I leave?"

Victor nodded. "Sure. Is it about—"

"Sort of," Juniper said, interrupting him.

Victor nodded again. "Okay. I'll send him your way."

"Thanks, sugar bean."

Not long after Victor left, her food was brought out by none other than Patroclus. "Victor said you needed to talk to me," he said, sitting in the chair directly across from her at the table.

"How good is your sniffer?" she asked.

Then she cut into her steak and took a big bite. The taste exploded on her tongue, and it was all she could do not to moan her enjoyment for all to hear. "My God, this is amazing. Every time."

"Thank you," Pat replied proudly. "What do you need my nose for?"

After licking sauce and butter from her fingers, Juniper dug into her purse and retrieved the bag, which she slid across the table to Pat. "Sniff that, if you would be so kind, and tell me what you smell."

"I'd rather not," Pat said, giving her a hard stare.

"Tori found it in the guesthouse," she explained. "We think it might belong to the murderer. I just want to know if you can pick up anything strange, like blood or something."

"Playing amateur sleuth, are you, June?" he asked, taking the bag.

"Something like that," she replied.

"The detective isn't going to like that."

"Sir Quacks-A-Lot can waddle his way back to where he came from for all I care. Did you know he shut down my Halloween party? Just like that!" She snapped her fingers to indicate the swiftness with which her fun had been destroyed.

"How terrible," Pat said, not sounding the least bit sorry for her.

Juniper knew it was a long shot to think the party wouldn't get cut short—there had been a dead body in her guesthouse, after all—but it didn't mean she had to like it. She took a drink of her soda and let the fizz burn away the irritation she felt at having Desmond Mallard be the one to ruin her fun. To Pat, she said, "Are you going to scent that thing or not?"

"Shouldn't this be in evidence?" Pat asked, one brow lifted.

"No," Juniper replied, narrowing her eyes at him.

After a short stare down, he cracked the zipper and brought the bag to his nose—and immediately gagged.

Juniper winced in sympathy. "Is it that bad?"

Pat immediately closed it and tossed it back across the table to her. "It smells like hot vinegar and rotten pickles with a side of lily of the valley. Good God, June, what the heck?"

"I didn't know!" she protested. "I could hardly smell anything."

Pat made a face. "As you know, my sense of smell is a lot keener than yours."

She nodded. "Yes. Thanks for risking your nose for me, Pat."

"Was that all you needed from me?"

Juniper chewed her piece of steak as she thought about that for a few seconds. "One other small thing. There was an altercation here a few months back between Dorella Smith and Hannah Peterson. Do you remember that, by any chance?"

Pat snorted. "Hard to forget two grown women catfighting."

"Sounds interesting. What happened?"

"It was a real humdinger. Started inside. Dorella was seated with Randy Jakes. He had the Tomahawk steak, usually does. If you ask me, he should lay off those if he doesn't want to end up inside one of his own caskets before his time."

"Wait… Randy Jakes from the funeral parlor?"

"Yeah. Dorella is dating him. Or was. Not sure if she still is. Anyway, Hannah came in and made a beeline for their table. Started calling Dorella all sorts of names."

"Names?"

"Yeah, apparently she didn't like that Dorella slept over at Randy's." Pat shrugged. "Kind of prudish in this day and age."

"No kidding." Juni filed away that little tidbit. Dorella was dating Randy from the funeral parlor where Hannah worked. Maybe Hannah wanted Randy for herself. Wouldn't be the first time two women fighting over a man ended in murder. "So then what happened?"

"They were disrupting the other customers in the dining room, so we kicked them out. They continued fighting in the parking lot, and Vic called the cops. Hannah was pretty mad about that, especially when we told them she was the one that started it."

"I'll bet. But no one got arrested or anything, did they?" Juni wondered if Mallard knew about this. Maybe he already had Dorella on his suspect list.

"Nah, the cops broke it up, we bagged up the rest of Randy's steak, and they went their separate ways." Pat pursed his lips. "Two days later, Hannah left us a bad review on Yelp. Can you believe that?"

Juni shook her head. "Vindictive."

"Exactly." Pat's eyes narrowed, and his expression turned hard. Then he shifted in his chair. "Do you need anything else?"

"No. But thanks a lot. You've been very helpful."

"Don't mention it," he grumbled, getting up and walking away.

Alone once more, Juniper slid the patch back into her purse and cut off another bite of steak.

That certainly had been enlightening. The patch smelled like sour food. Maybe whoever wore it liked fermented cuisine or something. And what about the side of lily of the valley? Perfume, maybe? Dorella did usually wear strong perfume, but Juniper wasn't exactly sure of the scent.

And Dorella and Hannah had fought. Maybe Dorella wasn't at her house earlier because she was at Randy's. But what was Hannah's beef about that? Did the two have a feud going on that had led to murder?

Juni had gotten a bad vibe when Pat talked about the Yelp review. He was clearly not pleased about it. Remembering those scratches on Hannah's face, she wondered if a bad review would be enough to make him kill.

But if Hannah was killed by Dorella, Pat, or Brandi, then how in the world had Hannah's body gotten into the casket that ended up in the guesthouse?

CHAPTER THIRTEEN

"*H*ot vinegar and rotten pickles? Probably formaldehyde," Victoria told her when Juniper explained about Pat's explosive reaction to the band patch. "Not sure about the lily-of-the-valley part, but why didn't you bring me back a plate? I've been in here writing all day. The last thing I thought about was food, but now I'm starving."

"You haven't thought to pay attention, either, obviously, or you would have noticed the takeout bag in my hand." Juniper raised her hand, and Tori reached for the bag.

"Yum." She pulled the bag's contents out and pushed her laptop aside. "But yeah, the smell is one I never forgot from science class. In eighth grade, our physical science teacher made us all dissect a baby piglet. We had to measure its entrails and brain and stuff. Or we were supposed to.

"I excused myself from class and stayed in the bathroom for the rest of the period every day after that until quiz day." She shuddered. "Paper, I can handle. Baby piggies preserved in formaldehyde? Not so much."

Juniper hopped onto the corner of the desk and pulled up one leg until she could wrap her arms around it just below the knee and hold it in place. The other, she kicked back and forth in a swinging motion. "So it's a preservative? Got it. But why in the heck would it be on a band patch? Do they use it in iron-on preparation or something?"

"I don't think so," Tori said around a mouthful of steak. "It's used in embalming fluid, so it probably came from the funeral parlor."

"Interesting. But maybe not. Hannah worked there, so maybe the smell is from her."

"Or the killer. Remember, Hannah worked on the accounting end. She might not have gone into the morgue part of the business. When I researched the funeral parlor for one of my books, I found most people avoided that place unless they had to go there."

"Yeah, I can see why. They keep the caskets down there, and I had to go to pick one out for the party. It's creepy."

"The patch doesn't really give us any good clues, then?"

"Au contraire." Juni slid off the desk and picked up her purse. "Before I went for dinner, I stopped by the library to do a bit of research on the public intronets."

"Juni, we have internet here," Tori reminded her.

"Yes, we do," Juniper agreed. "But I didn't want that on my browser history for Mallard to find. You know that rubber dubber is watching every move I make. He just doesn't like me for some reason. Anyway…" Juniper paused, dug in her purse, then pulled out a slip of paper and handed it to Tori. "Clear your calendar for tomorrow, girl. We're going to the concert in the park."

"Concert? Juniper, you know I'm in the middle of a pretty harrowing plot twist right now, and my mind is all caught up in figuring out what happens next." She shook her head. "I can't go. You'll have to get someone else."

Then, as if it only just occurred to her to wonder about this, she asked, "Why are you going to the concert? It's a local band and not even remotely similar to your usual eighties-hair-band tastes. What gives?"

"It's the band on the patch you found, and I think it might have led to some clues. The internet had pictures of Hannah's stepson's girlfriend with patches just like it on her jacket." Juniper told her about her internet search, finding the stepson and the girlfriend, and what she'd learned about the fight with Dorella and the bad Yelp review. "Dollars to doughnuts the girlfriend will be at that concert tomorrow, and I'm of a mind to have a word with her."

"And what about Dorella? That seems like a good lead."

"I have a call in to her." Juniper checked her phone just in case Dorella had called back or messaged her and she'd missed it. Nope.

Unease etched itself over Tori's face. "Juni, you know the detective will be upset, especially if you confront this girl in public. Besides, you have no proof. You can't accuse her of killing Hannah without proof."

Juni was offended. "Who said anything about confrontation? And I never said I was going to accuse her of anything, much less murder. As for Mallard, well, he doesn't even know about the patch or that the girlfriend had one. Why will he care if I chat up someone at a concert he won't even attend?"

"How do you know he won't be there?" Tori went back to her steak. She cut a thick slice and chewed, her eyelids slipping low as she savored the taste.

"Ha! Your duck man never had a day of fun in his life. He wouldn't recognize it if it kicked him in the keister. If fun walked straight up and introduced itself to that man, he would be confused."

Tori shrugged and tucked in for another bite. "You never know, Juniper. Stranger things have happened. What if he not only shows up but turns out to be their biggest fan?"

"A-hem."

Juniper turned toward the wall between Tori's office and the kitchen, where Jacobi stood, half-in and half-out of the wall. "What is it?"

"A couple of ducklings are parked just outside the perimeter wall, Ms. Juniper. Lionel said I should let you know to keep your conversation neutral because they probably have ears on?"

"Spies! Low-down, sneaky, nosy bunch of spies!" Juniper walked to the door of Victoria's office and called for Terrence, the butler in her employ who still had breath in his body and blood flowing in his veins. "Terry, I want you to go down to the perimeter wall and toss a bucket of something nasty over. Maybe they will have their windows down."

Tori snorted. "Very classy, Juniper. You might as well have told him to toss used mop water on the detective's men."

"Didn't I?" she asked. But then she narrowed her eyes. With a smile, she said, "You know what? Never mind, Terrence. I can handle this intrusion into our privacy myself."

She waved at Tori. "Later, gator. Good luck with your writing!"

CHAPTER FOURTEEN

*D*ressed to the nines, Juniper drew the attention of more than a few pairs of eyes as she meandered through the crowd of people here to see their favorite bands...or to endure the noise so their teens could have a good time.

Juniper didn't take the time to find out who else was playing, but with a name like Lyrical Larynx, the band was bound to be interesting if nothing else. She might even discover some new tunes to add to her large library of music.

But the band wasn't on yet. The stage was still being set up, and Juniper was scanning the crowd for a head of shocking pastel purple and white. She'd passed a few on the street, but none belonged to her suspect. She had no idea the color combination was so popular, although it was very pretty.

Finally, she spotted her quarry and managed to elbow her way over. She sidled up next to the girl, pretending to be just meandering in the crowd, then stepped right in her way while looking in the other direction.

"Oh, excuse me! I'm so sorry!" a feminine voice exclaimed. "I didn't see you there."

"It's no problem," Juniper said, pretending to regain her balance. She turned and smiled at Brandi.

Brandi smiled back and then promptly turned her attention forward, Juniper forgotten for the moment. Juniper chewed her lip for a second, trying to think of something to say other than "Did you kill Hannah Peterson?" because that wouldn't go over well. As it turned out, she didn't have to come up with an icebreaker, since Brandi did that for her.

"Who are you here to see tonight?"

"Lyrical Larynx," Juniper replied, glancing at Brandi to see how she reacted.

Her brows lifted slightly. "Wow, really? No offense, but you don't seem the type to listen to… well, that kind of music."

"I listen to all music," Juniper said, waving her hand about. "Old stuff, new stuff. Crazy stuff. I love music."

Brandi stared at her, clearly sizing her up. Her lips moved in a small smile that bordered on a smirk. "Seriously?"

Juniper laughed. "You don't believe me."

"Nope. Sorry. You just… kind of make me think of my mom, and she *hates* this kind of music."

"She probably needs to remember what it was like being a teenager. I'm sure she was into something her parents didn't like once upon a time."

Brandi snorted. "I couldn't tell you. The way she tells it, she was a saint."

It was Juniper's turn to snort. "That usually means she was into some stuff she doesn't want getting out."

"Really?" Brandi asked, arching one brow. "How do you know?"

"Because I know a few people like that.

Troublemakers growing up, boring people when they turned into adults. I don't know why people think they have to stop having fun when they turn a certain age. Life's not meant to be endured. You're supposed to live it. Like me," Juniper said, winking.

Brandi shook her head, but she was smiling. "I don't think my mom sees it that way. She thinks I should spend more time studying and less time having fun."

"Well, she probably means well. Wants you to have a good future. Studying is important too. What are you going to school for?" As if Juniper didn't already know.

"Nursing."

"Admirable. I could never do it. All those needles." Juniper studied Brandi to see if she reacted to the mention of needles, but if Brandi had guilt over killing Hannah with a needle, she didn't show it.

"Needles aren't bad once you know how to use them." Brandi shrugged. "I don't think my mom sees it as admirable. I get decent grades but not good enough for her. If she's not blaming that on the music, it's my boyfriend, who she also doesn't like."

Juniper tsked. That was nowhere near a confession, but it dinged a few bells in Juniper's brain. Troubled teen. Strict parent. Knew how to use needles. That was trouble, right there. "What's wrong with the boyfriend?"

Brandi sighed, her face losing some of its lackadaisical freedom from a moment ago, like she was remembering something unpleasant. "Nothing," she said, her tone implying there was, in fact, something. "He's just... She just doesn't like him. We had an argument about it, actually. He and I, I mean."

"That doesn't sound pleasant."

"It wasn't."

"Ms. Holiday. Fancy seeing you here."

Juniper's excitement for the evening soured like buttermilk in her stomach. Rolling her eyes, she turned to look up at Desmond and almost fell over. Instead of his usual suit and tie and police-issue trench coat, he was wearing a sweatshirt and jeans. She tried not to notice that he filled them both out quite nicely. He looked almost human.

"What are you doing here, Mallard? Don't you have anything better to do than follow me around?" She made a face. "Please, tell me you haven't imprinted on me. I can't deal with that. I didn't have children for a reason."

Desmond offered her a closed-lip smile. "A service to the world, I'm sure," he responded dryly. "As for why I'm here, I'm sure my reasons are much the same as yours, are they not?"

She narrowed her eyes. "I doubt it."

He chuckled.

Juniper turned to make excuses for Detective Mallard to Brandi only to find the girl had disappeared. Growling in the back of her throat, she glared up at Desmond. "You scared her off!"

"From you? I hope so."

"Funny. I was starting to get somewhere, thank you very much."

Desmond raised a brow. "With what, Ms. Holiday? Please, tell me you weren't trying to get information from her, because if so, you were doing an abysmal job."

"I was doing just fine, thank you."

He declined to reply.

Juniper sighed and crossed her arms. "Seriously, why *are* you here? I don't imagine someone as straitlaced as yourself actually enjoys this kind of music."

"What would you know about that? You haven't even heard them."

Juniper pursed her lips. "You don't seem the type."

Desmond smiled again, looking almost predatory. "You don't even know what kind of music is about to be played, Ms. Holiday, so I'll thank you to keep your opinions to yourself until you've been educated."

Juniper opened her mouth to argue when the band was announced, and the crowd roared with excitement. Wicked fast drumbeats landed, followed by bass so heavy she felt it in her organs, and then a screeching yell echoed through the speakers at such a volume that it made Juniper's eardrums spasm.

She couldn't hear Desmond's laugh, but she could see it in his eyes. He leaned down next to her ear, yelling to be heard over the music. "I won't say anything if you can't handle it, Ms. Holiday."

Juniper lifted her chin and turned on her heel to watch the show. She wasn't about to tuck in her tail and run from a little screaming.

As she focused on the band, she went over the conversation with Brandi in her head. One thing stuck out... For a girl whose boyfriend's stepmom had just been murdered, she didn't seem too upset about it.

CHAPTER FIFTEEN

*L*yrical Larynx, Juniper learned later, was what the cool and happening kids called a "screamo death metal band." Their music wasn't terrible, she decided, once she learned how to hear both the lyrics and the music without letting one overpower the other in her head.

Not that she would definitely add the band to her collection the minute she drove away from the concert, but she could deal with a few hours of it... unlike Mallard, who had disappeared shortly after the first set, she thought smugly.

"Wow! They were amazing!" Brandi Hulsey said. At some point during the concert, she had popped up by Juniper's side again and stayed there for the duration. "I thought you would cut out like that old guy, but you stuck it out. What did you think?"

Old guy? Juniper smirked and then cast a quick look around for Detective Mallard. He was standing over by the fence, watching her. He pointed two fingers at his eyes and then at her. The nerve!

"They were definitely different," Juniper told her. The security guards were herding people toward the park exits, but Juniper was of a mind to go in a different direction. "I could see touches of my usual preferences in their style, but they do belong in a class of their own. Do you know if there is merch available? I'd like to pick up a patch for my goddaughter."

Brandi shrugged. "Usually, but I wouldn't bother. I bought a patch at their last park concert, but it didn't stick, even though I followed the directions to the letter. You're better off buying from their website. The suppliers through there source much higher-quality stuff."

Juniper stared at the girl's crop top, her eyes

asking the question she almost didn't voice. "Where did you put it?"

Brandi laughed. "Not on this thing, duh! I had it on a hoodie. I left it at my boyfriend's, but…" Something flickered in her eyes, and she shrugged. "I'll probably never see that thing again."

With a tilt of her head, Juniper motioned for Brandi to walk out with her. "Bad breakup, huh?"

Another shrug. "Maybe. Probably should have been, but it was more just a big fight, really —uhm, not the physical kind, in case you were thinking that. We just had a really big argument."

"You wanted to see Lyrical Larynx, and he was more partial to Leo Sayer?" Juniper pretended to guess at the reason for their fight. To her surprise, Brandi laughed.

"Leo Sayer? You're hilarious. My mom used to listen to him, back in the day, but I'm sure Gage wouldn't know who he is. As for the argument, it was about his stepmom, actually. He was furious with her." The look in her eyes grew distant. "We both were."

Juniper blinked twice. Was that motive?

She'd have to choose her words carefully now. Brandi didn't know that Juniper had any knowledge of Hannah, and she didn't want to scare the girl off. She needed more information.

"I'm sure he will cool off. You have. Maybe this stepmom will apologize and all will be well again in no time," Juniper said. She certainly was fishing!

Brandi's eyes welled with tears, and she shook her head. "No. No, no, nope. Can't. She's dead now, you see. The police won't say who's responsible, but they are investigating her death as a murder."

"Oh, dear. I'm so sorry. Do the police have any clues as to who might have done it?"

"If they do, they ain't sharin'," the girl said. "But I'd love to know, you know? Ms. Peterson didn't deserve to die. She was a nice woman."

Juniper frowned. Murderers usually didn't describe their victims as nice—unless said murderers were trying to cover their tracks. She studied Brandi Hulsey as if seeing her in a new light. "You liked her?"

"Yeah. Was she overbearing, too strict, and a tightwad when it came to money? Every day of the week. But she knew what was right, and she stuck to it, no matter what."

"Was that why Gage was mad at her?"

"Yeah, he thought she was too strict, but she was trying to make him more responsible. Got him a job at the funeral parlor and made him go even though he thought it was creepy."

"But why did you and Gage fight, then?" They were not too far from the gate, and Juniper saw her car way off in the parking lot. Wait... was that Mallard leaning against the bumper? And who was he talking to? Why, it was Victoria!

Brandi shrugged. "I just thought he should go easy on her. In her own way, she was trying to do what was right for him, even if it was really old-fashioned. Might be for the best. Gage has a bit of a temper."

Aha! Maybe Brandi wasn't the culprit. Could Gage have killed his own stepmother? But how would he know where to place the needle to cause the embolism.? Brandi would know exactly where the artery was, but Juniper wasn't so sure whether Gage would. Maybe he'd been helping Brandi study. Come to think of it, didn't they embalm people by pumping formaldehyde into that artery? That would mean syringes and needles. Brandi had just said that Hannah made Gage get a job at the mortuary.

Now Juniper had another person to add to her suspect list, but she couldn't spend much time pondering if Gage could be the killer, because just then, she spotted someone in the crowd that made her heart lurch.

Dorella Smith!

Their eyes locked, and Dorella's widened in panic. Then she turned and ran. Juniper took off after her, leaving Brandi to make her way to the exit on her own.

Juniper could just see the top of Dorella's head as she weaved her way through the oncoming crowd. Trying to catch up, Juniper jostled and elbowed people, catching quite a few dirty looks and rude comments. Little did these people know she was trying to catch a killer! Dorella had to be the one. Why else would she have run away?

Up ahead, she saw Dorella take a hard left

behind one of the vendor tents that sold T-shirts.

Juniper put on a burst of speed and skidded around the corner in time to see Dorella leap over the tent stake. Juniper gave it all she had, sprinting toward Dorella, then leaped forward, arms out toward her quarry. She caught her by the back of the hair, yanking her head back. *Ouch! That must have hurt*, Juniper thought, as the two crashed to the ground.

Juniper was on top of the other woman in a second, holding her down to prevent her escape.

Dorella squirmed and struggled, trying to unseat Juniper. "Get off me!"

"Not until you confess!" Juniper ducked backward to avoid a punch to the face.

"Cut it out, Juniper! You're hurting me!"

"Like you hurt Hannah?"

"Huh? What are you talking about?"

"You know exactly what I'm talking about. I'm calling the cops, and they'll go easier on you if you confess, so you might as well tell me what happened and why you did it." Juniper had no idea if this was true. It probably wasn't, but she wanted to be the one to get the confession out of the killer before the duck man had a chance.

"All right, I confess! I was planning on keeping your money, even though I didn't do the gig."

"What?" That wasn't exactly the confession Juniper was looking for.

"You heard me. I was going to keep the money. Why do you think I've been avoiding you?"

"Umm, because you killed Hannah Peterson." Dorella had stopped struggling. Juniper leaned forward and sniffed. "That's a nice scent. Is it lily of the valley, perhaps?"

Dorella looked at her like she was crazy. "No. White Shoulders."

"Oh." That didn't mean that Dorella didn't wear lily of the valley sometimes, like when she was killing people and dropping band patches.

"Are you going to let me up?"

"What were you doing when Hannah was killed?"

Dorella sighed. "I had been out to eat with Randy. I came to the guesthouse like I was supposed to, but the cops were there. I didn't want to get involved, so I left."

She seemed to be telling the truth, but killers lied, didn't they? "So you didn't fight with

Hannah over Randy like you did at the steak house a few months back?"

"What? No! We weren't fighting over Randy then anyway."

"What were you fighting over?"

Dorella crossed her arms over her chest. "Let me up and I'll tell you."

"Fine." Juniper grabbed Dorella's wrist and pulled her up. She kept hold just in case Dorella tried to run off.

Dorella yanked her wrist away and brushed the dirt off her jeans. "I didn't kill Hannah. I didn't even see her that day. We avoided each other, usually."

"Because of the fight?"

Dorella wasn't even trying to run, so maybe she was telling the truth.

"Yep. Well, that, and we didn't really get along. Hannah was very straitlaced and liked to impose her puritan views on others. She didn't like that Randy and I spent the night together sometimes."

"And that was what you fought about at Rarely Done?"

"Yep. We were minding our own business, eating dinner, when Hannah came in and spotted us as the hostess was seating her. She came over and called me a tramp!" Dorella certainly did look mad enough to kill at the memory. "If you ask me, she had issues."

"Clearly. But if you aren't guilty, then why have you been avoiding me? Why did you run just now?"

"Well, first of all, you aren't the police. I've talked to them. And second…" Dorella grimaced. "I thought you wanted me to pay you back for the job, since I wasn't able to complete it."

"You ran because you didn't want to give my money back?"

Dorella nodded. Maybe Dorella wasn't the killer, but she sure seemed talkative. At the very least, Juniper figured she might get some dirt on the other suspects.

"Do you know anyone who might want to kill Hannah?" Juniper cut right to the chase.

Dorella snorted. "Who wouldn't? Honestly, I don't know her that well. Randy said she was harmless, but she sure could rub people the wrong way. Even her own stepson didn't seem very happy with her."

"I heard. Do you know him well? What

about his girlfriend?" Juniper reasoned that Dorella might have run into them at the funeral parlor. Brandi said Gage had worked there, and maybe she visited him. Did they have access to the embalming area?

"I met her a few times. Seemed nice. Gage is a little quiet."

"I hear Gage worked there. Did he work in the embalming room?"

Dorella shivered. "I wouldn't know. I never went near that place. It's in the basement and very creepy. That was one thing I had in common with Hannah. Neither of us went near the basement."

Juniper knew what she meant. When she'd met with Randy to pick out the casket, she'd felt the same way. The caskets were kept in the basement area. They were displayed nicely in a room, but still, knowing the dead bodies were just down the hall was a bit discomforting.

"I bet Gage and Brandi didn't mind going there, though. Kids that age sometimes like creepy places." If Hannah never went down there, then the formaldehyde scent from the patch likely came from the killer and not Hannah. But how did the killer get her down there and into the casket? Maybe the murder happened in the garage on the level above when the casket was about to be loaded in the truck for delivery?

"You're asking a lot of questions, but now I have one for you," Dorella said.

"What's that?"

"Are you going to make me give back the money for the Halloween job? It's not really fair that I couldn't perform the job because *you* had a dead body in your guesthouse. That's not my fault, and I could have booked another job, but I missed out on that since you didn't call to cancel ahead of time. So I think it's only fair I keep the money."

Juniper had actually already planned on letting everyone she'd hired keep the money. Dorella was right. It wasn't her fault. Well, unless she was the killer.

"Nah, you can keep it." The place had cleared out, and Juniper was out of questions for Dorella, so she turned to leave.

"That's it? You're not going to call the cops like you said?" Dorella asked.

"Nope." She didn't have any evidence.

"Juniper?"

Juniper turned back to look at Dorella. She was standing there with her hand held out. "What?"

"Do you think I could get the bonus you promised me?"

CHAPTER SIXTEEN

*A*n hour later, Juniper lay in the middle of her bed, staring up at the canopy of dark blue above her. Loki lay beside her, purring away. Finn was in the window seat, watching birds flit about in the trees. Ludo was sleeping in the bottom of the closet, nestled in a pink cashmere sweater that had been Juniper's favorite until the cat decided it was his private bed.

Juniper wasn't really sure who the killer was now. She'd thought Brandi would be the perfect suspect. Thanks to her nursing training, she must know where the important arteries were. But she'd acted the complete opposite of how Juniper imagined a murderer would, unless they were seriously meticulous and a dang good actor —neither of which she could imagine Brandi being.

Dorella was a good candidate too, especially with her previous argument with Hannah. But her argument about running because she wanted to keep the money was convincing.

The werewolves got a bad Yelp review, but was that any reason to kill? Then again, she'd seen how their personalities could change at the full moon. If one of them was really angry, they might have taken things too far. And it was Pat that had said the patch smelled of embalming fluid. What if that was a lie to throw her off track?

Then there was Gage. He'd argued with Brandi over his treatment of Hannah. Did he hate his stepmother enough to get rid of her?

Mallard hadn't seemed to think the girl-friend was of particular interest, either, when he'd interrupted Juniper and Brandi's chat. That irked her, but then she had to remember he didn't know about the band patch. "He probably doesn't even know Brandi was dating Hannah's stepson," she mumbled to herself, giving a ripping snort.

"I hope that noise came out of your face and not somewhere else," Tori said as she waltzed into Juniper's room as easily as if it were her own.

"It would serve you right," Juniper grouched, scowling at her beloved goddaughter. She sat up, propping her weight on her hands, and continued to scowl. "I saw you at the park, talking with Detective Downy-Butt. What the heck? You couldn't go with me because you were neck deep in plot, or so you said, but you can schmooze with the bad guy?"

"He's not the bad guy, June," Tori said, rolling her eyes. She huffed out a sigh, plopped down on the side of Juniper's bed, and began petting Loki's soft white fur.

"You're supposed to be my sidekick, Victori-no," Juniper said. "The Watson to my Holmes. The pea to my carrot. The butter to my mashed potatoes."

Tori looked at her for a long second, her expression neutral. Then, she said, "Has anyone ever told you you have a flair for the dramatic, Juniper Holiday?"

"Maybe once or twice," she replied, shrugging. "Your mom especially liked to point it out.

She often said I wouldn't know what to do with myself if I couldn't exaggerate at least three times a day."

Tori gave her a look. "She was right."

"Possibly. But we're not talking about my theatrics right now. We're talking about you and the duck man."

"Juniper, stop. I was getting information from him. That's all. In fact, I found out something about *you* that you didn't tell me."

Juniper frowned. "Me? Impossible. You know I tell you everything."

"You didn't tell me that you met with Hannah Peterson on the day she died. Detective Mallard thinks you might have been the last one to see her alive."

"What?" Juniper bolted upright. "He has that wrong. I was the first one to see her dead. Well, other than the killer and Fedora. But I didn't see her alive."

"Gage told the police that you were meeting with her to pick out the casket for the party."

"Hannah? No, I met with Randy for that. Dorella said Hannah never went down there near the morgue, so she wouldn't be the one I'd meet with for that... Wait... unless Dorella was lying."

"Excuse me." Lionel popped up through the floor, looking agitated.

"Lionel? What is it?"

Tori didn't seem at all perturbed that Juniper was talking to thin air. She was used to it.

"There's been a development. Jacobi was out in the garden looking over the herbs—I have no idea why, since he doesn't really do the cooking anymore. Anyway, he witnessed something come over the wall."

"Something? Like what? Was it over by the west gate, where we dumped something on the cops? I hope retaliation for that..."

"I don't think it's them. It was an article of clothing. Best for you to go look." With that, Lionel poofed out.

Juniper turned to Tori. "Someone tossed something over the wall when they thought no one was looking. Guess we better go see what it is."

"Maybe it's that pink scarf you've been going on about."

CHAPTER SEVENTEEN

*J*uniper and Victoria rushed to the old stone wall, where Lionel's ghost was swirling anxiously.

"It's over here!" He pointed at a shrub next to the stone wall.

"He says it's over there," Juniper relayed to Tori.

"I see it!" Tori reached into the shrub and held up a black hoodie. She shook it out and immediately gasped for air. "Take it! Oh! Phew! It smells atrocious!"

Juniper pinched the fabric between her finger and thumb, carefully holding the material away from her body as she did so. She clapped her other hand over her own mouth and nose. "OMG, what is it?"

Tori gasped and sputtered. "I'd know that smell anywhere. It's formaldehyde."

Juniper held the jacket as far away from her nose as she could. She didn't smell a hint of lily of the valley like Pat had said he'd smelled on the patch, but her sniffer wasn't as finely tuned as his. "It is? Why would someone dump it here?"

"Getting rid of the evidence?" Tori pointed at a darker round area on the jacket. Like a patch had been ironed on and had then come off.

"Brandi said she had a jacket where the band patch came off. Do you think this is hers?" Juniper turned to Lionel. "Did you or Jacobi see who tossed this here?"

Lionel gazed at the ground. "I'm sorry. We did not. Jacobi heard screeching tires and then came to look and saw the jacket."

"But why would Brandi throw it here?" Tori asked.

"I know why. To frame me. And it might not have been Brandi either. Dorella lied about Hannah not going into the morgue, but Gage said he thought Hannah was meeting me down there, so clearly, she did go there. I bet that was where the murder happened, and the murderer"—Juniper held up the jacket—"knows this jacket can incriminate them."

Tori frowned. "Dorella was at the guesthouse right before the body was discovered…"

Suspects swirled in Juniper's head. Whoever threw this jacket here might be trying to frame her. Would the werewolves do that? No, her money was on Brandi or Dorella.

"This is getting serious, and I think there's only one way to figure out who the killer is." Juniper started back toward the house. "We need to get to the scene of the crime. There might still be some clues left for us to find."

Tori grimaced. "You mean…"

"Yep. We need to get to the Peterson-Jakes Mortuary and Funeral Home, and we don't have any time to waste. If my guess is correct, the killer might already be calling a tip in to Detective Mallard so he'll come out to the property and discover this little piece of fake evidence."

CHAPTER EIGHTEEN

*D*esmond sat at his desk, the low light of the lamp pulling his focus into the papers stacked neatly in front of him. The subtle, rubbery thump of his pencil eraser against the desk acted like a metronome, keeping his thoughts in time.

This case was proving difficult for reasons he could not fathom. It should have been pretty cut-and-dried. Someone had been killed, and the body was deposited elsewhere to distract from the scene of the crime. People who weren't inclined to plot out intrinsic murders were usually very sloppy. Their fear of being caught made them overlook certain matters. Not to insult the intelligence of the Crescent Cove residents, but he didn't think anyone here was motivated and meticulous enough to make sure no evidence was left behind. But dash it if that wasn't how it looked.

His thoughts turned to events that had happened earlier in the evening, namely his little run-in with Juniper Holiday and later, her goddaughter, Victoria. Juniper had been playing at sleuthing, but he was willing to bet a month's wages she hadn't found out anything he didn't already know. Victoria, on the other hand, had surprised him. A piece of evidence had gone overlooked somehow in his initial sweep of the Holiday mansion's guesthouse. She'd been kind enough to bring it to him, bagged and tagged. He couldn't believe his people hadn't found it when they inspected the place. Did he have to do everything himself?

He'd done everything by the book, because that was how he operated. It was how he caught the bad guys. And yet an amateur—a civilian—had found evidence he'd been unable to see. He couldn't decide if the situation was humorous or ironic, but it was certainly sad, if nothing else.

At least it wasn't Juniper who had presented

him with the patch, he thought. That would have irked him for months.

A smile touched his lips. He wondered how Juniper reacted when Victoria told her she'd handed over evidence to him. He imagined she was none too pleased. That thought alone made his evening a bit brighter. But the case still had to be solved, and he was running out of time.

The sound of a door closing somewhere nearby brought him out of his head and to the present once more.

"You stayin' late again, sir?" Haverman asked as he came into view.

"It looks that way," Desmond responded, running his hand over his face. He suddenly felt very tired.

"Maybe this will cheer you up." Haverman tossed a manila folder onto his desk.

Desmond frowned. "What is it?" he asked, already opening it.

"The test results for the iron-on patch."

Excitement sluiced through his veins, and he eagerly scanned the papers before him, Haverman putting voice to everything seconds after Desmond was finding them out himself.

"I think there should be enough DNA to finally pin down our guy... or gal, yeah?"

"We can only pray," Desmond said.

"There was an anonymous tip too," Haverman said. "Person wanted us to check out the grounds at the Holiday mansion." Haverman shrugged. "Already been over it with a fine-tooth comb, but do you want me to send someone out?"

Desmond's brow quirked up. "Anonymous? Interesting. I guess you'd better check it out."

"I'll get right on it."

Desmond closed the file and stood. He clicked off the lamp and grabbed his jacket from the back of the chair. The tip was interesting, but he doubted a concerned citizen was suddenly trying to lead them to clues. Most likely, someone wanted to lead them on a wild goose chase.

But who?

He had the suspects narrowed down. Someone was lying, and he had a good idea who that someone was.

He glanced at his watch. It was after hours but not too late to pay a visit to the funeral parlor. And if his hunch was correct, he just might be able to catch the killer in the act of trying to cover their tracks.

"Juni, we shouldn't be here!" Victoria hissed in a stage whisper, which was completely unnecessary, since she was standing right next to her godmother, who was glaring at her for blowing hot air into her ear.

"It's not like we're breaking and entering. The door was unlocked."

Victoria glared at her. "That doesn't make it okay! We're here after hours! This place is closed to the public!"

"Live a little, hon." Juniper rolled her eyes, though it did make her a little nervous that the door had been unlocked. They'd waltzed right in, expecting someone to be there, but the lights were off, and the place was empty. She had to admit the viewing rooms with their open caskets were creepier than heck when the funeral home was empty and dark.

A familiar scent wafted out of one room, and Juniper stepped inside. There was a vase of flowers on a table. Lily of the valley. Had the patch gotten the scent on it from actual flowers? Did the killer handle the floral arrangements?

"Juni! This is no time to stop and smell the flowers!" Tori whispered.

With Tori gurgling her anxiety behind her, Juniper continued on her mission down the back hallway that led to an inconspicuous set of stairs to the basement. Whoever had killed Hannah must have been around the formaldehyde, and since the patch must have been stuck in the casket somehow, it stood to reason that the murder happened down there. As far as she knew, the police hadn't swept the area, so now it was up to her.

Turning a corner, she came upon a set of swing doors, the kind that had windows in them. Behind those windows, she saw a shadow, as if someone on the other side of them had passed by. She stopped, frozen, in the middle of the hall. There was nowhere to hide. She was caught for sure!

The door swung out, and Juniper swallowed the scream in her throat. The other person didn't. A half-gurgled yell filled the silence of the building as she and a teenage boy stared at each other, aghast.

"W-What are you doing here?" the boy asked.

Juniper could have said she might ask him the same thing, but what came out of her mouth instead was "Is that my pink scarf?"

The boy, who she recognized as Gage Peterson, looked down at his hands. It *was* her scarf! Juni flashed back to the Halloween party, remembering the teen dressed as the skeleton who was standing near the coat closet. It had been Gage!

"You took that from my closet at the Halloween party!" Juni accused.

But why would he take it, and what was he doing with it now? Then it came to her. He'd planned it all along. The jacket thrown into her yard was just the first piece of evidence planted, and the scarf was the second. That meant...

"You're the killer!"

Gage threw the scarf in her face and ran back into the embalming room.

Juniper batted the scarf off and rushed after him. "Tori, call the duck man!"

Gage slid a stainless-steel gurney between them, grateful that there was no body on it. He grabbed a saw from the counter and pressed the button, causing it to whir ominously.

Gage started to advance on her, holding the whirring saw out toward her. "I'm not going to jail."

Juniper held her hands up. Was he going to saw her to death? "You don't have to go to jail. I can help you."

Gage looked skeptical. "How?"

"Well, for one, I'm sure it was just self-defense, right? Tell me what happened."

"I didn't kill my stepmom!"

Juni's gaze flicked from the saw to Gage's face. "Then why are you threatening me with that, and why were you trying to plant my scarf here in the funeral home?"

"I, ahh.."

"And did you throw that jacket into my bushes?" Juniper planted her fists on her hips. "Why do that if you aren't guilty?"

A voice from behind startled Juniper. She'd been so focused on the whirring saw that she hadn't heard anyone come in. "I think I know why."

Juniper whirled around and saw Desmond Mallard standing behind her. Dang! That man knew how to ruin all her fun. "You got here kind of quick. I just told Tori to call you not even five minutes ago."

"I was already on my way. With my police resources and skills of deduction, I had already figured out the identity of the killer."

CHAPTER NINETEEN

*D*esmond grabbed the saw from Gage and pushed him down into a chair. Juniper had to admit she was impressed that the duckman had grabbed the saw as if he wasn't worried about getting his hand cut off. He'd done it all so quickly that Gage was now sitting in the chair, looking stunned, as if his brain was trying to catch up with what had just happened.

But Juniper wasn't going to let Mallard have all the fun. She leaned over Gage. "Brandi told me you argued with your stepmother, but you took it a bit further, didn't you? You physically fought with her. That was how she got the scratches on her face, wasn't it? Did she fight back? Did she try to stop you?"

"Stop it! Just stop!" Gage said. "You're right —we did get into it. All I asked was for Brandi to stay over after your party. She refused. She had some misguided set of rules. Told me it wasn't right or some medieval bunch of nonsense like that."

He put his head in his hands. "She was always doin' stuff like that, man. Always shootin' me down. Always makin' me do 'what's right' according to some guidebook she read or something. I don't know, you know? But it's makin' me look bad to my friends."

He leaned back in the chair and crossed his arms over his chest.

"How did she end up in the casket?"

"The argument started upstairs. I was putting the flowers into slumber room five, and she came in and picked a fight. I tried to walk away, honestly. I came down here because I figured she wouldn't follow me. She hated coming down into the basement."

"Yet you told the police she was meeting me down here to look at the caskets." Juniper remembered the lilies of the valley in the room upstairs. Pat had been right. The jacket did have that scent on it.

"I had to think up a reason for her to be down here other than fighting with me." Gage looked slightly contrite. "Sorry about lying."

"What happened next?" Mallard gave Juni a look that conveyed he was the one that was supposed to be asking the questions.

"We scrapped a little. I pushed her. She pushed me. I swiped her cheek pretty hard, I guess, but it was by mistake." He shrugged, but Juniper could see he did sort of feel bad about that.

"So you admit you hit your stepmother?" Juniper's obvious disgust earned another glare from Mallard.

"I didn't hit her. She pushed me, and I pushed back. She pushed harder, and I fell back into one of the tables and got some embalming fluid on my jacket. That stuff stinks. As I was flailing, trying to wipe it off, she came toward me again, and I scratched her."

"So that was the jacket you threw in my yard? Was it Brandi's jacket, the one missing the patch?" Juniper asked.

Gage's eyes widened. "It was hers. I don't know about any missing patch, though."

"That's because it ended up on the casket

somehow." Juniper glared at Gage. "The one you tossed your dead stepmother in after you killed her."

"No! Like I said, I didn't kill her. We were fighting, and I grabbed the first thing my hand touched on the counter." Gage gestured toward the counter he'd grabbed the saw from. A stainless-steel tray with surgical tools and syringes neatly lined up sat there.

Mallard's brow arched. "And?"

Gage sat down. "It was an injection thing. They use them during the embalming process. But there was nothing in it, I swear! They don't leave them around full of fluid. So I jabbed her with it just to get her away from me. It was empty! She should have been fine!"

Tears started to slide down his cheeks, and he kept shaking his head back and forth. "She should have been fine, but she—she just stared at me with so much disappointment in her eyes. Then she grabbed her head then her chest, and she hit the floor. I didn't know what to do."

Juniper snorted. "The numbers 911 ring a bell?"

Gage shook his head again. "It was too late

for that. She wasn't breathing. She didn't have a pulse."

"So you put her in the coffin to hide her?" Tori asked. Unlike Juniper's, her tone was gentle. Kind. Understanding.

He nodded. "I did. I thought someone else would find her, and they'd figure she had a heart attack and toppled in. You wouldn't believe how easy those lids fall shut. Everyone knew she was scared down here. And she really did have a heart attack, so…"

"But things didn't go to plan," Juniper said.

"I had no idea that casket was the one that was going to your party. I didn't find that out until I went to the party myself."

"So you left your dead stepmother in a casket and went to a party?" Juniper asked.

Gage sighed. "I had to make things look normal. But when I got to the party and saw the cops, I had a bad feeling. I crept over and looked in the window and saw her in the casket."

"And then you came up with the idea to frame me," Juniper said.

"Well, I figured the cops might look a bit too

closely, so I took something of yours to plant in the funeral home to prove you were here."

"And you told Detective Mallard I met with your mother," Juniper said.

"And threw your girlfriend's jacket into our bushes," Tori added.

Gage nodded. "I did all that, but those aren't real crimes. And my mom died of a heart attack, so that's not really a crime either."

"Afraid you're wrong there," Mallard said. "That empty needle that you stuck in your mother's artery was full of air. And since you pushed down the plunger, it caused an air bubble, which resulted in an embolism."

"Wait. What?" Gage's gaze flicked from Mallard to Juniper to Tori. "You mean I really did kill her?"

"Afraid so." Mallard pulled him up from the chair. "Looks like you'll be making a trip down to the station." He motioned for Haverman. "Read him his rights. Put him in the car."

Juniper turned to Mallard. "Well, it looks like this case is solved."

"No thanks to you. You could have gotten killed chasing after Gage in here. And I'm surprised at you, Tori." Mallard looked at

Juniper's goddaughter, who blushed and stared at the floor. "There's just one thing. That band patch. Seems to me my people should have found that. So I wonder, how did you end up with it? Perhaps you found it with the body before you called us, and you were withholding it? I could charge you for that."

Juniper gasped. "I did no such thing. We found it *after* you people packed up and left and gave it to you right away. Guess your crew isn't as good as you think they are."

Mallard studied her for a few seconds as if to decide whether she was telling the truth. "Maybe not, but there is one thing we're good at. We did find the killer."

CHAPTER TWENTY

$\mathcal{D}$ays later, Juniper could be found muttering to herself wherever she was in the mansion. The occasional "Ha!" could also be heard from time to time in whatever room she was in. Victoria wondered if she was talking to one of the ghosts, but something told her that wasn't the case. She would have full-on conversations with them. What she was doing now was more like just grumbling to herself, like if she were remembering a conversation from days ago and only just now thought of the perfect comeback.

Those moments were the worst.

She left her godmother alone, though, her own time now taken up exclusively with finishing her newest gothic romance. Sometimes, her thoughts would slip back to Gage Peterson, and she'd take a moment to contemplate how such a young person could be driven to murder over something so small. But then, she hadn't been raised with such strict rules as Gage had. She could imagine he might have felt like he was suffocating beneath the weight of his stepmother's moral code.

"Oooh, suffocation," Victoria mumbled to herself and jotted down a quick note on the sheet of paper next to her. "That's going in the next book."

Meanwhile, in the west wing of the mansion, Juniper sat in an overstuffed armchair, facing one of the many windows in the room. All three of the cats—Ludo, Loki, and Finn— were with her, Finn taking the coveted spot on her lap, and she idly stroked his silky silver fur as she aired her grievances aloud to the only creatures who would sit still long enough to listen to her.

"'We did find the killer, Juniper,'" she mocked in an exaggeratedly deep voice. "Can you believe him? I'd just found Hannah Peterson's murderer, and he had the *gall* to take that away from me! Grr! That really burns my biscuits. It does, it does.

"I was a step ahead of him the whole way, and he stole my thunder because he was the one with the badge. I bet he was a snot-nosed brat when he was a kid, always running to tattle on the other kids when they did something he thought they shouldn't."

Juniper at least had Gage on her suspect list when she went to the funeral parlor that night. Okay, maybe she wasn't exactly sure that he was the killer. She did have a few other suspects, but still. She got there first, so she should at least get some credit.

Finn meowed and stretched before settling again into sleep. Juniper continued to pet him. "Don't tell anyone this, but I guess I can't actually be mad at him. He was doing his job, after all. I was just doing it 'cause I wanted to throw a spoke in his immaculate wheel." She shook her head. "Nobody should be that put together all the time. I can't imagine any woman would want to put up with that for any length of time."

"Detective Mallard is here to see you, ma'am," Lionel intoned, floating up through the floor at about the same time Desmond walked into the room, followed by Terrence.

"The detective is here to see you, Ms. Juni," Terrence said, almost lazily.

"I can see that," she said. "Thank you, Terry."

He nodded and walked away without another word.

Lionel sniffed. "Appalling."

"You could teach him some things," Juniper muttered as he began to sink back through the floor.

"I would ask what you said, but I don't think I want to know," Desmond said as he made his way across the room to where she sat.

"I was talking to Lionel, my ghost butler. He doesn't like the way Terrence does things, so I told him he could teach him a thing or two if it got on his nerves so bad."

Desmond looked at her like he wasn't sure whether to indulge her or ignore her. In the end, he chose the latter.

Juniper lifted a brow. "What brings you by? I would think you wouldn't want to step foot here again. You can sit down, by the way. The furniture won't eat you."

"Thank you, no, I'll stand. I'm not going to be here for very long."

"You're leaving town?" Juniper felt hopeful.

"Your home, Ms. Holiday. I'm staying in the Cove for a while yet, I'm afraid."

"Drat."

He smiled. And it wasn't in a sarcastic way. It was genuine. Juniper almost couldn't believe it.

"I came by to thank you," he said.

"Thank me?"

He nodded once. "Yes. Without you finding that patch, we wouldn't have been able to solve the case so quickly. I still don't understand how we missed it. I'm sure we looked under the rug."

Juniper stared at him a minute, her lips pursed as she mulled over what to say. "I have a confession to make, Desi. I didn't actually find the patch. Victoria was the one who found it."

Finn reseated himself, Loki stretched in the corner, and Ludo ran over and sniffed Mallard's shoes.

The detective stared at the cats. "These cats were in the guesthouse. They might have moved the patch around. That could explain why we didn't find it." He glanced up at

Juniper as if she'd instructed the cats to steal evidence.

"They do like to bat things around. What other explanation could there be?" Other than incompetence, but Juni didn't want to say that. The detective had come to thank her, and she didn't want to seem ungracious.

Mallard nodded. "Anyway, just wanted to let you know that it's appreciated."

"Is this… is this a truce?"

"A tentative one, I'm sure."

"That's probably best," Juniper said, nodding slowly.

"Well. I should be going," Desmond said. "Will you give my thanks to Miss Cooper for her involvement?"

"I will."

He inclined his head. "Thank you. And, if I may be so bold, I hope our paths never cross in that manner again, Juniper Holiday."

Juniper smiled. "As long as no one else dies on my property, they won't, Duck Man."

He smiled again and shook his head. "Good day to you," he said. Then he turned and walked away.

Juniper shook her own head at his retreating

back and then turned her attention to the window once more. The sun was starting to set. The trees were mostly bare this time of year, but it wasn't quite cold enough for sweaters yet. Then again, this far south, it wouldn't get that cold till after January. Christmas would already be over, and they'd be heading toward Valentine's Day.

Oh, but before any of that, they had to get through Thanksgiving.

Thanksgiving…

She frowned. Dang it. In the interest of keeping the peace between herself and the authorities in Crescent Cove, should she invite that twerp to Thanksgiving dinner?

Heaving a sigh, she set Finn aside with a bit of effort and hotfooted it out of the room. "Duckmeister! Hold on a second!"

****

Thanksgiving doesn't turn out exactly the way Juniper planned but the biggest surprise is for Detective Mallard …. Find more in Thanksgiving Dinner Death.

Sample of Chapter 1 Below:

The Holiday mansion was currently a madhouse. Thanksgiving was the next day, and there were dozens of people in Juniper's kitchen, running around like chickens with their heads cut off in their haste to get everything ready in time. Naturally, Sabrina couldn't be expected to cook for hundreds of people on her own, so Juniper had called in

Bite-Sized Catering to help out with the spread, and Sabrina was ordering them around like a general on the battlefield. Her mother would have been proud.

The savory aroma of roast turkey mingling with cinnamon and spices made Juniper's mouth water. Golden-crusted pies had been set on the table to cool, and the helpers were chopping and mixing to prepare some of the food ahead of time.

Up until a few minutes ago, Juniper herself had been helping, too, but she could sample the fare only so many times before she was ordered out. Which, honestly, was totally fine with her. She needed some fresh air anyway.

Before she could make it out the door, Jacobi, her ghostly cook, stopped her. "Why do you continue to let that woman butcher my family's recipes, Juniper Holiday? Do you know how long it took us to perfect them? Hmm?"

Juniper had to bite her tongue quickly in order to keep from saying the exact wrong thing, which would set Jacobi off. The last time she'd spoken without thinking very carefully about her words, he'd thrown a ghost-sized tantrum, and everyone had suffered for it. She still couldn't eat lemon meringue pie without tasting salt.

She cleared her throat. "A very long time?"

"Indeed," Jacobi affirmed, puffing his chest out with pride. "Every ingredient was carefully chosen in order to perfectly complement the dish." His bushy brows suddenly lowered over his ghostly eyes. "And that woman is ruining everything!"

Juniper sighed to herself. He had to be talking about the dressing. "Jac, honey, I'm sure Sabrina didn't mean to butcher the recipe," she said, "but you have to understand that she's under a lot of pressure right now. She's got dozens of people in her kitchen who don't know how she runs it, and you shouldn't blame her. Besides, you should at least try her improve —er, changes to your treasured recipes before you complain they're ruined. That's fair, ain't it?"

Jacobi continued to stare at her in ghostly anger, his form slowly bobbing up in down in front of her. Then, with a great sniff, he began to rise toward the ceiling, glaring at her the whole way—and there was a good fifteen feet to float—until he disappeared.

At least he didn't make the food explode, she thought, rubbing her temples.

Remembering her original plan, she scooted down the hall to the foot of the main staircase, taking time to admire the holiday décor as she went. She hadn't gotten too carried away because she planned to break out the Christmas decorations right after Thanksgiving, but she wanted the place to look festive for the dozens of guests who would arrive for the meal.

Displays of pumpkins were set about in various places. Big pumpkins, small pumpkins, orange pumpkins, white pumpkins. It was quite a display. The fireplace mantels had been draped in garlands of fall leaves in bright red, yellow, and orange, and colorful flower arrangements completed the look.

"Tori!" she yelled up the stairs, which had been draped in a fall-themed garland, "I'm going into town. You need anything?"

Three sets of feline eyes blinked back at her. The housecats, Loki, Luna, and Finn, had been banished from the kitchen and dining areas for the dinner. No one wanted cat hair in their gravy. The cats were quite annoyed at this, and Juniper could see the recrimination in their luminescent gazes. She knew she had better be on her guard, because she was sure they would find some unpleasant way to pay her back.

"What are you going for?" Tori yelled back.

"I've been banned from the kitchen."

"Ha! Bring me back a coffee and I'll love you forever."

"You've promised me that dozens of times already."

"And I'm promising it again. Make it sweet, Juni!" Tori warned. "Plain is nasty."

"All right," Juniper called back, shaking her head and rolling her eyes as she made her way out. Her dear goddaughter liked those sticky-sweet concoctions from WitchRoast Café, whereas Juniper preferred a bold, dark roast with a hint of cream and a touch of sugar.

At least Tori didn't like stump water, which was what Juniper called any coffee that wasn't so strong that a spoon could stand up in it on its own. She would have had to disown her for that.

Pealing out of the drive in her pretty little GT, the radio blasting "Killer Queen" by Queen, Juniper made the trip into town.

The smell of fall was heavy in the air, touched with a hint of winter waiting around the corner, and Juniper breathed it in as she got out of her car and headed into the warm, cozy interior of the cafe. The smell of coffee and pastries was strong as she stepped inside, and she nearly moaned at the delicious aroma.

"Hey, June!" Quincy Gilbert greeted her from behind the counter.

She raised her hand in a wave. "Hey, Quince."

"The usual?"

"Yep," she said with a nod. "And Tori wants something sweet, so maybe that unicorn-looking drink on the menu for her."

"You got it," he said with a chuckle.

Juniper moved to sit at one of the tables next to the window to wait. Not long after she'd sat down, a young woman with long, dark hair took the seat across from her and slid something across the table to her.

"Put that on," the girl said, lifting her hand to reveal a small sterling silver ring fitted with a black stone.

Juniper raised her brow. "Why?"

"Because it will protect you," the girl said, her dark-blue eyes steady as she gazed directly into Juniper's.

Juniper raised her other brow. "Why do I need protection? And who the heck are you?"

The girl smiled. "You know at least one secret of the Cove, Juniper Holiday. That alone opens you up to tragedy and danger." She pushed the ring closer with the tip of her finger. "Put it on. You'll thank me for it later."

And then she was gone. No name. She just got up and left.

"She wasn't bothering you, was she?" Quincy asked as he came over with her drink order.

Juniper looked away from the window to peer up at him. "Who was that?"

"Her name's Halen," he said, his brows furrowed. "She's new to the Cove, but she's certainly memorable. She goes around offering protection charms and cryptic words of advice then leaves before anyone can get anything straight out of her." He shook his head. "I wouldn't take anything she told you to heart, June."

"No worries there," Juniper said, taking her drinks and standing.

"Oh, that's a nice ring. Where'd you get it?" Quincy asked.

Juniper frowned. She didn't remember putting on a ring. But when she looked at her hand, the ring Halen had pushed her way sat, pretty as you please, on her left pinky finger.

S ignup for my newsletter and be the first to know about new releases, plus I'll send you a free cozy mystery story!

https://leighanndobbscozymysteries. gr8.com

MORE BOOKS BY LEIGHANN DOBBS:

Cozy Mysteries

Juniper Holiday Cozy Mysteries
***

Halloween Party Murder
Thanksgiving Dinner Death
Who Slayed The Santas?

Mystic Notch
Cat Cozy Mystery Series
* * *

Ghostly Paws
A Spirited Tail
A Mew To A Kill

Paws and Effect
Probable Paws
A Whisker of a Doubt
Wrong Side of the Claw
Claw and Order

Oyster Cove Guesthouse
Cat Cozy Mystery Series
***

A Twist in the Tail
A Whisker in the Dark
A Purrfect Alibi

Moorecliff Manor Cat Cozy Mystery
Series
* * *

Dead in the Dining Room
Stabbed in the Solarium
Homicide in the Hydrangeas
Lifeless in the Library

Silver Hollow

Paranormal Cozy Mystery Series

***

A Spell of Trouble (Book 1)
Spell Disaster (Book 2)
Nothing to Croak About (Book 3)
Cry Wolf (Book 4)
Shear Magic (Book 5)

Blackmoore Sisters
Cozy Mystery Series

* * *

Dead Wrong
Dead & Buried
Dead Tide
Buried Secrets
Deadly Intentions
A Grave Mistake
Spell Found
Fatal Fortune
Hidden Secrets

Kate Diamond Mystery Adventures

3 Bodies and a Biscotti

Brownies, Bodies & Bad Guys

Bake, Battle & Roll

Wedded Blintz

Scones, Skulls & Scams

Ice Cream Murder

Mummified Meringues

Brutal Brulee (Novella)

No Scone Unturned

Cream Puff Killer

Never Say Pie

Lady Katherine Regency Mysteries

***

An Invitation to Murder (Book 1)

The Baffling Burglaries of Bath (Book 2)

Murder at the Ice Ball (Book 3)

A Murderous Affair (Book 4)

Murder on Charles Street (Book 5)

Hazel Martin Historical Mystery Series

***

Murder at Lowry House (book 1)

Murder by Misunderstanding (book 2)

Sam Mason Mysteries
(As L. A. Dobbs)

***

Telling Lies (Book 1)
Keeping Secrets (Book 2)
Exposing Truths (Book 3)
Betraying Trust (Book 4)
Killing Dreams (Book 5)

Romantic Comedy

***

Corporate Chaos Series

In Over Her Head (book 1)
Can't Stand the Heat (book 2)
What Goes Around Comes Around (book 3)
Careful What You Wish For (4)

Contemporary Romance

***

Reluctant Romance

Sweet Romance (Written As Annie Dobbs)

Firefly Inn Series

***

Another Chance (Book 1)

Another Wish (Book 2)

Hometown Hearts Series

***

No Getting Over You (Book 1)

A Change of Heart (Book 2)

Sweet Mountain Billionaires

***

Jaded Billionaire (Book 1)

A Billion Reasons Not To Fall In Love (Book 2)

Regency Romance

* * *

Scandals and Spies Series:

Kissing The Enemy
Deceiving the Duke
Tempting the Rival
Charming the Spy
Pursuing the Traitor
Captivating the Captain

ABOUT THE AUTHOR

USA Today best-selling Author, Leighann Dobbs, has had a passion for reading since she was old enough to hold a book, but she didn't put pen to paper until much later in life. After a twenty-year career as a software engineer, with a few side trips into selling antiques and making jewelry, she realized you can't make a living reading books, so she tried her hand at writing them and discovered she had a passion for that, too! She lives in New Hampshire with her husband, Bruce, their trusty Chihuahua mix, Mojo, and beautiful rescue cat, Kitty.

Find out about her latest books by signing up at:
https://leighanndobbscozymysteries.
gr8.com

If you want to receive a text message alert on your cell phone for new releases , text

COZYMYSTERY to (603) 709-2906 (sorry, this only works for US cell phones!)

Connect with Leighann on Facebook
http://facebook.com/leighanndobbsbooks

This is a work of fiction.

None of it is real. All names, places, and events are products
of the author's imagination. Any resemblance to real names,
places, or events are purely coincidental, and should not be
construed as being real.

HALLOWEEN PARTY MURDER

Copyright © 2022

Leighann Dobbs Publishing

http://www.leighanndobbs.com

 Created with Vellum